Prune, Plant, or Plunder?

By Jessica Gardener Lee

Copyright @ 2011 by Jessica Gard'

D1369695

Edited by M.E. Hart

Cover is an original pencil and pastel portrait by Madeline Panichelli and Cookie C.

Table of Contents

Summary

Romance and intrigue on the Main Line...

She was born with a metal trowel in her hand; he was born with a silver spoon. Is their relationship sustainable?

Readers with an interest in gardening will enjoy the many references to horticulture in this suspense-filled romance.

Local references to the storied suburbs of Philadelphia, the Main Line, and Valley Forge, as well as environmental awareness, permeate the novel.

This is the first in a series of "Main Line Romance" stories based on an unforgettable group of locals. Enjoy!

About the Author

Jessica Gardener Lee co-founded an environmental club at Lower Merion High school in the fabled Main Line of Philadelphia, and she is a Master Gardener on hiatus in suburban Philadelphia. Jessica has a Master's Degree in Reading and Language Arts from Millersville University and a Bachelor of Arts from Brandeis University with a double major in English Literature and Cultural Anthropology. She has taught English Literature, English as a Second Language, and Reading, and has also worked as an assistant registrar at a college on the Main Line.

Acknowledgments & Dedications

I wish to acknowledge my fearless editor, M.E. Hart, for taking time from her busy schedule, for her nitpicking the story with a fine-tooth comb, and for always believing in this project.

Cover art acknowledgments go to Madeline Panichelli and Cookie C., and I credit you both with bringing my vision to life.

Lancaster County inspirations came from Debbie, a dedicated educator.

Thank you to Mildred Lester for sharing the story of her life and for all of her knitting and patience.

Thank you to the Chakov family, especially Mindy and Michael for your encouragement. Becky, for your encouragement and help early on.

To Lower Merion inspirations such as classmate Jacqui Kluft for being an inspiration with her environmentalism and to Mrs. Haas, Mr. Fisk, and English teachers everywhere. And Sudie Herdman- keep on gardening!

To the community garden organizers for putting up with me and my crew of little ones.

Lastly, thank you to my husband and sons, for their grace in dealing with my frequent escapes to the computer room to work on this story.

Dedications

This story is dedicated to the memory of my inspiring aunts- Helen, Barbara, Rose, Lena, Angie, Dorothy and Pauline - for your grace, determination, and fortitude, and for appreciating that sometimes the simplest things in life are also the finest.

Chapter 1 - First Impressions

"You never have a second chance to make a first impression."
Carolina Albero to her grandchildren, Jimmy and Isabella

Partially concealing Max's broad chest was an incongruous dark blue apron covered in golden French hens. On his head was a large white chef's cap. Wynnewood's most famous homegrown talent was hiding in the kitchen. Attempting to pass off his social avoidance as a "good deed," he escaped the crowded engagement party by sequestering himself with the marinating steaks.

Max was disappointed to be away from the ocean view from the deck of his white Roman coliseum-like property on Long Beach Island, the Ivy family's vacation compound. He had planned to spend most of his hiatus from his lucrative, but sometimes chaotic, TV job at the beachfront property.

Mostly, Max just wanted to be outdoors, in the fresh air, which he did just about any chance that he got. The outside was his favorite place to be, but the kitchen was a distant second. He knew his way around kitchens from his new town, Los Angeles, to his home town of Wynnewood, Pennsylvania. Making people smile through his unique creations was one of the ways that Max found joy and pleasure.

His father, however, did not think it was appropriate for the only son of a Main Line old-money family to be a culinary artist, landscape artist, or any kind of artist whatsoever.

Most of the wealthiest folks in the famed outskirts of Philadelphia had amassed their fortunes in pharmaceuticals, the defense industry, and finance. Following the financial downturn of the last decade, only a select few of the wealthy along the Main Line were still from old money. The rest of the people of privilege, according to Mr. Harrison Alexander Ivy, were merely transplants or upstarts.

During his want-for-nothing upbringing, Max was frequently reminded of the uniqueness of his and his much older sister, Julia's, pedigree.

Because of his hallowed place on the social register, and his outstanding personal characteristics, his future was already written in stone. His parents expected him to be a CEO, a U.S. senator, or a diplomat, like his paternal uncle. They put up with some of Julia's eccentricities, but they expected more from Max because he would perpetuate the Ivy name into the new millennium.

Much to the chagrin of his meddling parents, Max ended up in a much different line of work - one that usually involved planting, pruning, and on occasion, picking.

But on the day of his favorite niece, Charlene's engagement party, he was simply marinating. With his escape to the solitary confines of the kitchen, Max mostly hoped to avoid his sister and her cohorts, the cheerleaders from the class of '82. As they clucked and gabbed while cavorting to have him settle down with their unattached daughters (and, in a few cases, even unhappily married ones), most of whom had the personalities of – fittingly – potted plants, Max was happily ensconced in the safe, although a bit stuffy, confines of the kitchen.

His solitude was interrupted by a creak of the white kitchen door, and a giggly redhead expressing her gratitude. "Oh Max, it is so sweet of you to cook for us. I always enjoy your grilled steaks, what ever do you marinate them in?" asked Charlene, his spitfire niece who escaped from the party with a glass of champagne in hand to bring to her kitchen helper.

"It is a secret, my dear," he said, as he gladly took the champagne. "Is the grill all revved up?"

"Jimmy's out on the patio, he says it is good to go," replied a giddy Charlene.

At that very moment, a gaggle of barking hounds enveloped the kitchen. Jimmy's two playful but determined canines burst through the kitchen and went right for the perfectly seasoned, juicy, raw steaks. Just as Max was about to grab on to one of the leashes, it got caught on his leg and dragged him to the other side of the kitchen.

A striking beauty with long dark hair and porcelain skin was trying to gain hold of the other dog's leash, which had attached itself to the leash that was dragging Max.

Max found himself tangled and twisted up together with the unknown dream woman. This continued, due to the out of control mutts, until their bodies were pressed snuggly up against each other.

"No, Rex and Lucky, that's not your food! Put down those steaks!" Isabella commanded. Suddenly looking up at Max, donning a smile, she felt a need to apologize for the ruckus. "I was trying to take the dogs outside for a walk, but they made a beeline for the kitchen. I'm so sorry!" stammered the shaken up beauty.

At the sound of a possible hysterical female, Max's valet-henchman, Cyrus, lurched out of the obscure nook between the kitchen and the study. "Is there anything that you need, sir?" he asked.

Max was not particularly minding the firm breasts that were pressing against his chest. It was sort of nice the way she was squirming, too.

Max felt that this kitchen escapade really should be playing itself out, instead of being so rudely interrupted. Perhaps he should give his bodyguard the signal they have set up for when he wanted not to have his body guarded. However, his dedication to his niece made him want to save the party from the invasion of the canine snatchers. He wanted Cyrus, who was hired for his keen problem-solving abilities, quick thinking in the line of fire, and dominating physical strength, to save the cookout. The beautiful brunette, whoever she was, would just have to wait.

"Cyrus, I would sure like it if we could salvage the steaks. If not, could you go to the nearest butcher shop and purchase some new ones?" Max requested of his trusted employee.

"It would be my pleasure, sir," said Cyrus, as he exposed his well-concealed knife and freed his employer and the young lady.

"Oh, and Cyrus," Max asked, "Please take a trip to the pet store and buy new leashes for these blasted mutts. Jimmy is out on the patio at the grill and can fill you in on what type to purchase. And could you please return these beasts to whatever room they were romping around in before they thought our steaks were their kibble?"

"Certainly, sir, and is there a specific type of steak you would like me to get?" he asked.

"Ask Jimmy about that," said Max. "I need to get cleaned up; I've got champagne all over my shirt."

And with that, Max took off his apron and polo shirt to reveal perfect abs, bulging pectoral muscles, and a torso that smelled ever so much like sparkling bubbly.

At that point, it dawned on him that his lovely new acquaintance, and erstwhile dog walker, was staring at him. Accustomed to garnishing female attention, he smiled broadly. And, therefore, was totally shocked when the young lady in question demurely excused herself and ran out of the room.

Chapter 2 - A Prickly Assignment

"Every rose has its thorns."
Gardener Dan to his daughter, Isabella

Isabella ran through their assignment and frowned, a tiny line coming visible in her flawless, pale complexion. It was a quirk of fate, a twist of irony, and a total pain in the butt that an outdoorsy, landscape artist was given a bone-china porcelain face to adorn with the highest SPF she could find. Currently, she was sporting #30 waterproof sunscreen, under foundation with an SPF of 15. Her hair, however, could take the heat and never frizzed, leaving her with little need to fuss with her long black locks.

Her cousin Jimmy, a true dear in every sense of the word, had asked her to help design his future wife's yard of her dreams. In addition to designing and installing the garden plan, she would help get Charlene to the site and surprise her.

Isabella asked if there was a formal garden plan in the works. Jimmy smiled that wry smile he got when he was about to beat her at chess, or Parcheesi, or any other of the myriad of childhood games they played as youngsters in their grandmother's kitchen.

"Style and substance," he explained, "will be our *modus operandi* here."

Isabella was used to the goofy things Jimmy would say. But she also got exasperated at trying to figure out their meaning. Usually, she had to go back and rethink about what the main point was in the preceding conversation, and work forward from here. So, where were they? Oh yeah, something about how he was totally in love with style-conscious Charlene - and willing to do anything to make her feel at home in his and his daughter, Lacey's, strictly suburban abode. And what was this about a designer? Did they want her to be their designer?

"Well," Isabella asked, "we all know my designs have a great deal of substance, but where is all of this style coming from? We all know it isn't from you." She had been ribbing him on his clothing choices ever since he wore a skinny tie to his prom, and, since he often put pens in his pocket, he was usually known for his ink stains more than any sort of appreciable style.

"Of course, I leave all of that color palate stuff to Charlene, although she's been trying to get me to retract the tips of my pens…"

"Wait a minute; didn't you say this is to be kept a surprise from Charlene?" Isabella asked, rapidly growing impatient with her cousin's circumlocutions. "How are we to get her unique brand of style on the project if she is kept in the dark?"

"Well," replied Jimmy, "where do you think she got such a great way of putting a look together, cousin?"

He explained that Charlene's mother, Julia, was helping to plan and pay for this surprise. "It was her idea! You met her at the engagement party, what did you think?"

Isabella recalled a voluptuous 40-something woman, wearing a very current-looking tight beige-colored knitted sweater set ensemble, and a long gold chain, dangling to her midriff. She was really out there, and taking no prisoners as she complained about the stemware pattern that her daughter picked out as being too basic and drab.

"Your future mother-in-law, while surely stylish, may not have the same sort of taste as your bride. In fact, I think she is the type that would ask me to put in stone fountains on top of motion detector fountains, on top of fountains on top of spring-fed fountains. You know, *that* type." Isabella had occasionally complained about customers requesting overly exuberant designs.

"Jimmy," she said, "even *I* can tell that they totally have opposite tastes and styles, and I wore hiking boots to the prom." Actually, Isabella realized that she really enjoyed Charlene's taste in elegant clothing. For a 23-year-old, Charlene's cocktail dress had seemed very cool and retro. It reminded her of the "Jackie O" style from the early 1960's that Isabella had seen on the History Network. "This is turning into the gift from hell, Jimmy. I can just see it, fountains over fountains..."

"Yes, well even Julia realizes that she is out of her element in the garden. So she had this great idea to bring her baby brother in on the project. You know, Max, the guy who covered you in Worcester sauce the other night..."

"Oh, and that's where we get the lack of substance in this equation, huh?" she responded.

Jimmy knew that Isabella didn't hold anything back. She was a woman who held her ground. But, he really didn't know how she would react to the idea of working closely with Max on a project. They had a history, and not a great one. Max was a fellow Lower Merion graduate who had been in Hollywood, doing one of those before-and-after fixer-upper shows, and he had a habit of telling bad jokes and all of that. But, the bottom line was that he was someone that Isabella couldn't stand back in high school.

From being raised around the sort of cold and impervious people like Harrison Ivy, Max had built a tough shell around himself, which resulted in a sometimes uncaring veneer. However, Jimmy knew from his fiancé, that Max was just all sweetness and light when it came to her. She had gone through rough times back in her teens, and fallen in with a group of losers. It was Max who recognized the signs of what was going on and insisted she be pulled out of private school and put into public school so she could meet a new group of kids.

Jimmy knew that Max was not a bad guy; he just basically played one on TV.

Jimmy then begged to get her to help. "Please, Isabella, please? It might be fun. If you can see past the bad jokes, he's really not a bad guy. Won't you consider working with Max on the design?"

Before he got to actually groveling, he remembered that he needed to make her seem important in the process, too. It wasn't all about Max and his Ivy League touch. "I would never think of putting something together like this without the Albero landscaping touch." That was an understatement. He desperately needed Albero in the mix to keep things affordable. Jimmy had agreed to pay for half of the project's total cost in plants and materials. However, he was hoping that with the free designing help and with Isabella's help supervising the budget, plus her connections with the local nurseries and supply houses, to keep to his budget.

Isabella was prepared to do anything and everything to make this a winning and world-class surprise wedding and house-warming present for her favorite cousin and his off-beat, but adorable bride. There was nothing more invigorating than using one's God-given talents to enrich the lives of the people she cherished, thought Isabella.

However, it would be a challenge to her patience, grace, and composure to work with a knucklehead who, in high school, had been the bane of her existence. Max was, and always would be, a complete no-neck chowder head, as she thought of him in high school, regardless of all of his fame and his Ivy lineage. As her father, Dan, used to always say when they discussed human nature, "A tiger never loses his spots."

Chapter 3 - Is the Project Sustainable?

"We were here before there even was a "Who's Who" register." Camille Ivy explained their social significance to her children, Max and Julia

The next day, at an outdoor café of his choosing, Max was led to his table by a buxom hostess. She was hoping to get his autograph, and maybe a phone number.

"Are you waiting for anyone else in your party?" she asked expectantly. She was hoping that it was another buff male celebrity, and not a date.

"Yes, a young lady. We'll be working on a project and need space. Would you mind clearing the table so we can put down some folders and such?" said Max.

"Certainly, can I get anything else for you?" With this she leaned in, showing her ample cleavage to her advantage.

Max nonchalantly replied, "Two glasses of water would be great." He was hoping the restaurant employee would take the hint and chill out a little. It got doggedly tiring being pursued all the time. He was here as a favor for Jimmy; he was curious about who he was meeting. The outdoor lunch meeting had been hastily arranged, and Max wasn't really sure what it was all about.

Jimmy had asked him to keep this meeting a secret, said he had a favor to ask of him. He had said that there would be a landscaping colleague meeting him here, a young lady. Max didn't know what it was all about, but, at least he was able to have this meeting outdoors.

His lunch companion abruptly stopped in front of his table, put out her hand, and said, "Hi, I'm Isabella, Jimmy's cousin."

She had her dark hair up in a scrunchy, with a Phillies hat on top, no makeup, and was wearing casual clothing. Despite the laid back, casual attire, she was stunning. Max would recognize the doll who had pressed up against him with the pooches for the rest of his living days. Here she was, but, the question is, why?

"I am so sorry, again, for ruining the first set of steaks," Isabella apologized. "I was just trying to take those dogs out for a walk, and they smelled the meat in the kitchen. Guess your steaks are as good as Jimmy says they are."

"Oh, you didn't try the replacements, or are you a vegetarian?" Max asked.

Isabella thought about how she had to leave the party because she had champagne and dog drool all over the new dress she had purchased expressly for the engagement party. The dress, her only nice outfit, was now sporting stains in some rather prominent locations. Embarrassed by this topic, she said, "I ate the chicken." She was eager to get past the subject of their mid-kitchen collision and on to the gardening project at hand.

"So, are we going to do it on camera?" the beautiful brunette in the purple tank top and frayed jeans inquired.

"Um, by *it* you mean?" asked Max, who was suddenly feeling very warm around his collar area. The humidity must be bothering him, he thought.

"The landscape project, the big reveal, Charlene's dream garden," she uttered, as if he was daft and didn't know why this meeting had been arranged. After a very long silence, Isabella interrupted the silence with a question. "You don't remember me from Lower Merion, do you?"

All of a sudden, he sat rigidly at attention. "What did you say your name is, again?"

He started thinking, but no, this couldn't be that overly serious girl they used to tease the heck out of in high school? Perplexed at how the long-legged lovely in front of him, with the shiny locks and porcelain skin had the same name and graduating class as a veritable wallflower, he was silent. He would have remembered those legs, and that skin. She must have been a transfer student, a foreign exchange student, maybe a former mute…

"Isabella Gail Albero, class of 1995, stage crew on *Grease*…" she listed, as if reading from underneath a yearbook photo.

"Nope, not ringing any bells," he said, as he got ready to order a few drinks to get the party rolling. As he was trying to find the waitress, getting annoyed that it was taking so long, she tried to steer the conversation back to the gardening project.

The waitress finally took their lunch order, and it seemed time for Max to get to the bottom of this dilemma. Speaking of bottoms, he thought, she probably had a really nice one.

"So, I have to confess, Jimmy didn't exactly fill me in on this meeting, what's up?"

Expecting him to be an ignoramus, she slowly summarized the project, showed him preliminary sketches of the site, went over which plantings should be kept intact, and some of her early ideas.

As he heard that he was going to have to work, not just play, with this serious-minded broad, he thought at least he would have a chance to execute some top-notch greenery in his hometown. His agent really wanted Max to generate some good PR during his hiatus, so, this will help his career in the long run. His good mood returned.

When Max took a look at Isabella's preliminary designs, he let out a yawn. Trying not to dash the hopes of someone so clearly an amateur, he said, "This is a very tried-and-true traditional landscape design. While there is nothing wrong with that approach," countered Max, "it isn't very exciting."

Isabella tarried by asking Max if he actually stayed awake during his classes, or slept through them like he did in high school.

"I see that you are a bit defensive, but there is no need to take this feedback personally," replied Max. "You may know how to garden, but you are just going to have to defer to my expertise on landscape design. I am a world-renowned expert with a degree…"

As he droned on about his degree and his experience, she decided to knock him down a peg or two, one of the specialties that she had developed in working in a male-dominated industry.

"Max," said Isabella, in a calm and even tone, "I am going to speak slowly so that even you can understand. Your education doesn't make you in any way superior to me when it comes to gardening. Even you can't buy talent, or common sense."

"I'm sensing some hostility here; is there something that I missed?" grumbled a confused and startled Max Ivy. He was used to being popular and coveted. His landscaping opinions were very much in demand because of his worldwide television exposure. He was a recognized expert in his field.

Isabella soldiered on, "I see I have your attention. A professional either makes a garden that is going to work for the customer, or they create a future minefield. Homeowners have to be able to maintain the landscape over time. Practicality is important. Here's a pen, why don't you take notes, Max?"

To humor his lunch companion, Max assumed note-taking posture. Instead of writing down the word "practicality," however, he started a pen and ink sketch of Isabella. He was enjoying how the flares of anger where making her eyes light up and sparkle.

"The next topic," Isabella explained, in a professorial tone of voice, "is sustainability. We want our designs to help the ecology, not deplete it. Using native plants, avoiding chemical fertilizers, these are ways to keep our ecosystem in check. Am I getting through here? Do I need to speak more slowly? You did study sustainability in college, right?"

When Max did not respond to Isabella's question, she decided to just go all-out in her assault on his gardening ethic. "I was talking about sustainability, you studied that, right? Or was that just one of the many lessons you got out of through family donations to the university? Did you actually have to go to classes? Were you really born with a silver spoon in your mouth?"

At this point, Isabella was absolutely sure that Max was not paying attention, and she was just about ready to say something, when she looked at his sketch pad.

"Did you ever see me play football at Lower Merion?" Max asked. "I had a great play against Radnor that made the high school hall of fame; I think people still talk about it today. Well, that is the mother of all rivalries, you know, Radnor and Lower Merion. It is the longest continuous rivalry in the United States, you know."

"Yes, I am aware of the rivalry. No, I can't recall ever seeing you play, that wasn't my scene. Speaking of scenes, what are you drawing?" She pivoted around in her chair trying to see his drawing, which he was trying to hide from her, quite unsuccessfully.

"Just a few more minutes on the drawing, please. I've always been good with my hands, on and off the football field. Here, take a look." Max studied Isabella's eyes, waiting to see the astonishment register as she viewed his artistic creation. It always gave him a little buzz to see the reaction that his drawings had on the opposite sex.

"That's rather good," she commented, noting the life-like flare of anger in her nostril and the sparkle of her eyes. "You're quite talented at portraiture."

"Thank you. I took several years of drawing in college, too, and I stayed awake for each and every class."

She was now quite embarrassed for having questioned his credentials so thoroughly. Maybe he isn't such a bad guy, she thought. If only he would keep his mouth shut.

"There were some interesting still-life and nudes, those were really some great apples, I used to love to draw those…peaches," Max grinned as he said what he thought was a hysterical description of a prominent part of the female anatomy.

Realizing that she had been delusional, and that clearly Max had not matured one bit since high school, Isabella decided to get the discussion back on track.

"Anyway," she interrupted, "let's get back to the project. I'd like to explain what it is that Jimmy and Charlene need from us. We are to do a fun, flowing space with flowers, veggies, and space for Lacey to run around."

"Now, which one is Lacey, the dog or the daughter?" Max quipped, as he uttered what he thought was a hysterical and irreverent question. This was the very sort of quintessential joke for which he prided himself.

However, he saw an expression of sheer disgust on Isabella's face. That's when he knew that she was one *major* serious-minded broad, despite her lascivious lips and voracious appetite. He enjoyed watching her devour her chicken salad sandwich on a croissant in record speed. He wondered where the food went as he took furtive glances at her toned and svelte physique. She might have the face of an angel and the body of a temptress, but he wasn't going to get anything from Isabella except a stern lecture on the proper use of mulch.

Patience, thought Isabella, take a deep breath. She thought about how her cousin Jimmy was overcome with romantic notions and promises, and how he wanted to make these dreams come true for his beloved fiancée, Charlene. Even if it meant tangling with the likes of Max, she would do anything and everything in the name of true love. Her mother would expect nothing less of her.

"I suppose that I should also fill you in on Jimmy's suggestions for the overall style of the project," Isabella said, in a professional tone. "I think I need to establish that we are going for a specific fine gardening style of Charlene's beloved Manicleer. That was where they got engaged, you know. Charlene wanted to get married there, but ceremonies are not allowed. It is a professionally landscaped pleasure garden from the early 1900's which is open to the public. I've been examining the site to determine what we can adapt to the suburban residential landscape. She absolutely would love to have a yard like Manicleer. This would be a dream come true, and there's absolutely no reason why it can't. But, then again, they have six on-site full-time gardeners to keep the place up and running. We have to make a design that can withstand the test of time, and Jimmy's ineptitude with hand-held tools and, God forbid, anything involving rotary blades!" She shivered at the notion of her cousin using a mower. "Perhaps we can use slow-growing grasses in the lawn; there are some new varieties available..."

"You really didn't try the steaks at the party?" Max was showing his lack of interest in Isabella's ideas for the gardening project. To Isabella, it seemed like Max's arrogance had no bounds. However, the word "steak" created some enticing imagery in her mind. Visions and sensations of Max pressed up against her in Jimmy's kitchen flooded her a bit senseless.

"Um, can you get over it already? I don't eat red meat. It is bad for the arteries. Can we talk about Charlene and Jimmy and this garden, please?" she fibbed. There was nothing she loved more than red meat, even if it was not particularly politically correct. And, don't even get her started on the subject of sausage. She loves it!

"Yeah, sure. Don't get all testy, I'm just on vacation and love to cook. Oh, and I did hear about her attempts to get married at Manicleer. She tried every trick in the book to get her way," chuckled Max. He thought about his spitfire niece battling windmills for her romantic ideals (and devotion to high style). It was just like Charlene to hand him a glass of champagne right before he got tangled up with Isabella. Memories of that afternoon enveloped Max, and he was trying to recall what they were talking about so he could get back in control of the conversation and the project.

"Well, she's one determined person when she sets her sights on something, or someone. Did you hear about how she and Jimmy met at a Phillies game? She climbed over two nasty Yankees fans so they could sit together and cheer on the fighting Phillies!" said Isabella. She was in a giddy mood from discussing something as wonderful as true love.

All at once, several rabid Max fans came over to their table, and asked him for autographs. It was an unfamiliar thing for Isabella, but clearly Max was accustomed to the intrusion. As the slightly inebriated fans started to get a bit rowdy, a very tall, muscular man in a suit came out of a nook in the bistro and said, "Excuse me, I see that you have your autograph. Can I ask you to move along please?" The fans weren't happy, but quickly departed.

As Cyrus dealt with the fans, Isabella's mind was free to wander. She remembered what Jimmy had said about the mysterious man with the blade who had freed her from Max's forceful embrace. She had called Jimmy to thank him for a wonderful time at the engagement party, and apologize for leaving so early. She had gone home and attempted to treat the stains in her dress, to no avail.

"You've got to be kidding, Jimmy," she had groaned over the phone. "Chowder Head has a bodyguard?"

"Chowder Head" was just one of the many nicknames that Isabella and her best friend, Jade, had coined for Max, and the spoiled-airhead jocks in high school. Max, though, always seemed to be at the head of the pack.

"Charlene said you and Max were kind of tangled up," said a mildly buzzed Jimmy on the phone. Just a little champagne always did him in. "I hope Max doesn't think you are one of his rabid fans, coming up with some sort of ruse to get your hooks into him." Jimmy knew that Isabella was giving chastity a try, and probably the least likely female on the planet to come up with a hare-brained scheme such as the dog leashes getting tangled. However, he could not resist the urge to tease his favorite cousin.

Isabella, completely shocked that anyone could even think of such a thing, said, "I'll have you know, Jimmy, that it was your rowdy dogs who got me in that tangle. It was getting stuffy at the party, and I didn't know very many people. All I wanted was a bit of fresh air, taking the dogs for a walk seemed like the perfect solution."

"Well, cousin, you have that in common with Max. You are both addicted to fresh air. But, he's sort of famous, so women chase after him. I guess it is the combination of his being on television plus his rakish looks."

Max took a minute to observe Isabella, as she appeared to be daydreaming. A furtive wish that she was thinking about him, pressed up against his warm body, swirled in his mind. Blue-collar types usually didn't get his blueblood heart thumping; it must be all this romantic talk about the dream garden or something.

Hoping to change the subject from all of the romantic talk, Max inquired, "May I ask you something?"

She looked up and they made eye contact.

"Have you ever seen my television program?" he asked, with no sort of filter. He was completely unabashed about regaling her with his accomplishments. After living all those years with Harrison Alexander Ivy, he had learned that there was nothing more noble or more grounding than achievement.

Typical, thought Isabella. He's always thinking about himself, except when he's talking about himself, or looking at himself in the mirror. Not that the image in the mirror was anything to be shy about. Max was one of the most physical, robust, sensual men she had ever met. His deep, low voice, healthy and hearty laugh, and sparkly merriment around his eyes made him resonate within her.

Because she was usually bone-tired in the evenings from a very physical garden installation or renovation project, Isabella rarely had a chance to watch television. However, she occasionally tuned in to this particular program to see what an environmental mess Max was making in the garden.

Homes on the Move was a popular prime time home improvement show, featuring a perky, perfect blonde host named Candy. After the big reveal, the transformed homes were always to die for. The dire predicaments of the homeowners were heart wrenching.

"Yeah, my friends and I make a drinking game out of it," she quipped, sure that the irony in her voice would convey the sheer absurdity of the lie.

However, the part of *Homes on the Move* that secretly got her heart thumping was the last segment before the renovation was complete. This was when the tired and worn landscape was reborn. She always tried not to recognize Max as he transformed the landscape with his "Ivy League" touches, and just imagine that he was just any old actor. This was easily achieved, as she was so engrossed in the renovation projects. However, she was mostly shocked at how little concern Max had for sustainability, keeping maintenance low, and other current themes in landscape design.

"I really dig that!" replied Max, who was finally feeling like he was back in "the zone" and not being kicked off some sort of reality show. She had treated him like a loser, but now he was back on top. *Homes on the Move* would make a great drinking game. "So," he asked in a seductive voice, "every time I take off my shirt…you do what?"

"I retch," she wanted to say, but it would sound immature. She searched for an appropriate response to his Neanderthal-like comment.

"I take out my rosary beads and start praying for the environment," she quipped. This is it. She was hoping that this would be the end of their meeting, the end of his involvement in the garden project for Jimmy and Charlene, and that she could go to a desert island, sit out in the sun, and sip from daiquiri glasses with little umbrellas in them. He didn't even realize the value of using native greenery!

By this point, a frustrated Max was willing to say or do just about anything to get Isabella to rescind her hold on this project and to let him finish it in peace. As a looker, she was all that and a bag of chips. But, as a partner on a design project, she was way too uptight. A plan quickly formed in his mind. A career landscaper like Isabella would be too busy in the summer to leave for the shore at the last minute; she probably went from paycheck to paycheck by the look of her clothes and her shoes, which were quite shabby. She needed the income from her job, and she needed to leave him alone.

"Oh, I just realized, if we are going to work together on this project, you'll need to come out to Long Beach Island for about a week. There's plenty of extra room at the old family compound. I'm spending a week around here to appease the parents, and then it is off to LBI. We would need a whole week or so there to get these disagreements worked out," Max contended. He waited sheepishly for the expected response. Gosh, he really could be clever, he assured himself gleefully.

Isabella had been putting off taking some warm-season vacation time for several years now. She usually had a lot of downtime during the winter, since they didn't get many calls for tree work until the spring. The idea of a beach, especially a very exclusive one, and luxurious lodging, was particularly appealing. Besides, being the boss' daughter had its perks. When it came time to ask for a scheduling favor, she had a life-long connection with the management.

The waitress cleared the coffee cups, and took a big long look at Max, practically devouring him with her eyes.

"Absolutely," said Isabella. "I'll get all my notes together and finish examining the site. When do we leave?" she asked. Enjoying the startled look on Max's face, she realized that it was quite fun to see him squirm.

Yeah, Isabella realized, spending time with that Ivy guy wasn't going to be too bad, as long as he allows her do the garden planning. If they steered clear of their high-jinxed past, and concentrated on the project, everything will be fine. She recalled how he had tripped her in the cafeteria and she almost dropped her tray of spaghetti all over the floor, and she shuddered. And, high school wasn't even the half of it. The Ivy family had been bullying her family for generations, since the exalted Ivys her dad and grandfather worked for thought of gardeners as second-class citizens. What ever got Max into the plant world, anyway, she wondered?

Chapter 4 - Bad Blood Between the Albero and Ivy Families

"Never judge a book by its cover or a spring bulb by its smell."
Professional Gardener Dan to his daughter, Isabella

"Look, you live in a town as long as I have, you know things about people," said Dan, still trying to understand why his daughter didn't enjoy the landscape renovation dream project she was undertaking.

Remembering how kind Mrs. Camille Ivy had been during his wife's terminal illness, Dan recalled a very caring matriarch. She had been very flexible and toned down her demands on his time at the estate, looking the other way when a few of the weekly tasks were left undone. "If Max is anything like his mother, he's a fine young man. He comes from good stock."

"Good stock, Dad? They fired you and sent us out in the middle of a hot afternoon without any place to live and we had to scramble to find an apartment, and you were stuck inside that…"

"That was his father. Alexander Ivy was always looking for a way to get rid of me. When that $500 dollars went missing, it was reason enough to get the 'gardener who thought he was above his place' out of there," he said. Plus, Dan thought, Mr. Ivy was miffed that Max, for whom he had high aspirations in the business world, was so interested in listening to the old gardener describe how to prune bushes and the proper combination of soil amendments for a good planting hole. But Dan thought better of sharing his memories of Max with is daughter. He was always rather sure that it was Max who had pilfered the $500 from his dad, and he didn't want to sour his daughter on her new partner for this project. Besides, there were other things that had happened back then that he didn't want to have her getting into. Lots of memories, good and bad, were buried at the estate.

"Well, I was happy to move on at the time, anyway," admitted Dan. "I know you loved the carriage house, and it was really cute in its own way, but I was itching to start my own landscape company. You know that, right Pumpkin? We wouldn't be where we are today, as a company and as a family, if we stayed on the estate."

"Dad, you talk about it like it was a plantation or a reservation or something, it was really nice. I remember the ponies…"

"And, do you remember that old man Ivy wouldn't let you play with the other kids, or even take the bus with them to school, because he didn't want anyone to think that you were a part of that family?" Dan countered.

"I didn't want you growing up thinking of yourself merely as 'the help' and I wanted to get into the landscaping business as more than a mere gardener. Now, I own my own company and you, my darling daughter, are my best employee. And because of your dedication to this company, you have earned some vacation time that is long overdue. Please, take Max up on his idea for you to go to Long Beach Island for a week so that you can complete the garden plans."

"I remember when Harrison first bought that place. It is like a miniature White House on the sand, right off the beach, and you can see the bay and the beachfront. I never was there myself, but Cook would give us the scoop every Monday when they returned from their weekend excursions. It will give me peace to know that my daughter is there as a peer, as an invited guest, and not as part of the staff. Makes me feel like everything I've planted all these years is yielding great fruit, okay?"

"Sure Dad," replied Isabella, "But just so we're clear - Max is a real knucklehead, just like he always was in high school."

"Just never judge a book by its cover is all I'm saying," said Dan, as he reached over to point to the new herb seedlings they had painstakingly grown from seeds in their greenhouse. "Pumpkin, be sure to water those transplants with the chamomile tea and fish emulsion I mixed up over there. It will prevent them from dampening off."

Chapter 5 - Sharon Rose's Dying Wish

"True love waits; promise me you will, too?"
Sharon Rose Albero to her daughter, Isabella, on her deathbed, 1989

Isabella had seen her mother lose weight rapidly, decline in energy and vitality, and become a shell of her former self, all in a matter of months. Cancer, in all of its manifestations, is a cruel and vicious opponent.

At twelve, Isabella was a budding beauty, but she was also very shy and socially awkward. She felt much more comfortable pruning a rose bush than talking to the popular kids at her middle school. Seeing her mother's decline had been a real shock to her, and she was not completely able to accept or absorb what was happening. Her father, Dan, was her rock through the whole ordeal.

As her mother beckoned her to the sickbed with a wave, a very imploring expression came to Sharon Rose Albero's eyes. She said, "Look at me. Look at me. Please. Wait. Promise to wait."

"Wait for what, Mom? Mom, please tell me what I am supposed to wait for." Isabella had tears in her eyes as she tried to gather the gist of this important promise.

Dan whispered in his daughter's ear, "Say yes, Pumpkin."

"Yes, Mama, I'll wait."

"True love waits," Sharon Rose explained, and then she left for the next world.

Despite the devastating loss of her mother at such a tender age, Isabella stayed strong. She wanted to be brave, she didn't cry any more. She kept her feelings bottled up inside and soldiered on. On the topic of "the promise," Isabella had every intention of waiting for whatever it was that her mother was asking of her.

Dan considered explaining it fully to the twelve-year-old Isabella, but he waited until she was 16 to have "the talk."

As Isabella grew into young adulthood, the immensity of that promise revealed itself.

Chapter 6 - More is Lost

"Someday you can become a U.S. senator, but not one of those mediocre state senators - you are from old money."
Harrison Alexander Ivy to his grandson, Max, upon his high school graduation

It was 1990, and Isabella walked home from the camp at the township playground, where she was a junior counselor. She wanted to tell her father about a particularly difficult camper, as Dan was always able to help her problem-solve.

Instead of finding her dad, however, she found the disheveled son of the mansion invading her turf, her inner sanctum.

It was not the first time that Isabella had seen Max at the garden shed, but she was curious as to why he was sitting down on the ground, instead of a chair, and then she got closer, and quickly saw why. Frat boy knucklehead was totally trashed! He started banging his head against the wall and saying over and again, "It can't be true, it can't be," and he seemed not at all in control of himself.

Isabella soon forgot why she had gone out to the shed, probably to tell her dad about something. She quickly went back to the carriage house, and only 20 minutes later was told that she needed to pack up all of her earthly possessions, as it was time to move on.

Her dad was not talking or saying anything other than that they had to get out, find a new place, and leave nothing behind.

She was glad she had her suitcases ready from her weekend trips to see her grandparents in their Overbrook Park row house. It was from her grandmother that she had learned how to cook Italian food and proper grooming for a young girl, and all of that girly stuff she couldn't garner from her otherwise terrific dad.

With bags packed and no clear plan, they set out in the heat of the afternoon for an adventure that was 10% perspiration, and 90%

inspiration. Dan had to think fast on his feet, a character trait that had served him well while he maintained the 12-acre grounds at the Ivy estate for the past 15 years. He had learned a lot from his father, who was the estate groundskeeper before passing away at a young age, probably from exhaustion.

Dan was the outdoor problem solver at the Ivy estate. If it wasn't groundhogs, gophers, or ground ivy, it was dealing with the occasional riff-raff and hangers-on that would come to see what all the architecture magazines and local society rags had written up as the most extraordinary estate on the whole Main Line.

While it was a crisis, he was able to keep his calm and write down a list of possible places to crash for a night or two with Isabella and their belongings in tow. He had always taught Isabella that writing down lists was the best way to deal with a troubling dilemma.

There was always his parents, but Dan did not relish the idea of staying overnight in "gossip town," as he called Overbrook Park. The neighborhood was a working class, tight-knit community. Once the "yentas" and "nonas" found out that eligible Dan was looking for a place to stay, he would be invited for lasagna by every hopeful future mother-in-law. Plus, he didn't want his parents to worry. They didn't need the aggravation, and he didn't need the hassle.

Dan's brainstorming soon yielded fruit. He remembered the name of a friend from his church who was the superintendent of a building in Ardmore, Ned Blake. Ned had mentioned that sometimes there were available rooms at the building. With a few phone calls, and all of his and Isabella's worldly belongings in the trunk of his pick-up, they moved into one of these vacancies, a two-bedroom apartment in a building next to the Ardmore train station.

Soon, he was entrenched in town life. Dan enjoyed being able to walk to the farmer's market, and he could take the train anywhere, never needing to pollute the earth with his truck unless he needed it for work-related projects. Plus, Isabella could even walk to school. This made it the ideal next step.

For Isabella, however, the new apartment was a far cry from the open land and greenery to which she had always been accustomed. Secondly, the train schedule would be permanently engraved upon her subconscious mind. It was almost like a party trick how Dan and Isabella would be able to rattle off the schedule to the city and back, and sometime his mom would call him instead of checking the Amtrak schedule. Pretty soon, however, she got used to the sounds of the train, and they no longer kept her up at night. The disappointment of suddenly being ordered off the Ivy estate, however, did.

The rent was going to be due very soon, so Dan asked his friend if the landlord would consider swapping landscaping on his rental properties in exchange for rent and utilities. The deal was struck, and with the good recommendation from his friend, he was able to also get some additional landscaping jobs here and there in the area.

At first, he was using the garden tools that were in the basement storage at the apartments, but it was soon clear that he would need his own tools, trucks, and even helpers. And with that, Albero Landscaping took off. Truthfully, when word got out that the second-generation gardener from the Ivy estate was out on his own, there were many who clamored for his attention to their properties. And word traveled fast about Dan's yen for turning a mediocre yard into an Eden-like oasis.

Chapter 7 - Time to Vent

"Men are mortal, diamonds last forever."
Julia to her daughter, Charlene, upon seeing her new engagement ring

After the stressful lunch meeting with Max, Isabella wanted to vent. How dare he be so darned handsome and so wrong about the environment at the same time?

While Isabella's best friend, Jade, would be at work at this time of day, this just couldn't wait.

Isabella took a windy back road to get out to the film studio, fuming about Max the whole way.

The receptionist at the Conshohocken movie studio where her friend worked as an assistant producer and video editor looked up and smiled. "I tried the peat moss alternative you told me about, Isabella, and it worked great. I'm so glad you told me about the peat bogs taking thousands of years to regenerate, that's unbelievable."

"Great, Nancy. It's nice to see you. Is Jade around?" Isabella asked, trying not to sound too desperate to see her friend.

"Sure, I'll let her know you're here. She is always working so hard and could probably use a little coffee break. You're good for her. If she had it her way, she'd be here 24/7 making movie magic and skipping meals."

Drinking coffee in the break room and resisting the tempting donuts, Jade asked what this impromptu visit was about.

"You're working with Max Ivy, of the Wynnewood Ivy's?" Jade mockingly drew out every syllable in a mock-old-money tone. "That's great, right?"

Realizing that Isabella was bent out of shape at the idea of working with her former nemesis, Jade quickly saw what her BFF needed from her, and switched to scorned woman tone.

"I can't believe he doesn't remember us. I mean, we were the ones on the stage crew who had the idea to use real motorcycles down the aisles, which was so dramatic! Remember how exciting it was when those Harleys revved up? Wow! Max Ivy is home to visit. Do you think he might remember me? I was more noticeable with being the only person of color on that production. Gosh, it has been forever since that fun cast party at the end of the show." It was hard for Jade to hide her enthusiasm about the local man turned national celebrity, renowned for his good looks. "He sure was a smooth Danny, though, I'll give you that much."

Jade was referring to Max's starring role in the school musical, *Grease*.

Isabella heard where the conversation was headed - something about washboard abs and pectorals, and did he have a personal trainer? She tried to steer the conversation towards the gardening project, "The point is, we've got to work together on this project, and we have a history that he doesn't even remember." Isabella explained.

"Well, Isabella, you were always hiding behind your glasses and your braids and your plant zones and petunias. We're in zone six, right?" Jade asked, trying to steer the conversation towards a safer topic, and the climate zone numbers, which serve as guides for what to plant and when, was a safe topic. Isabella didn't have a good track record with men, mused Jade. She didn't have much of a record at all. It was more like a blip on the radar. But, she did like her plants!

"Well, I know I didn't stand out, but I did live on his property. It just proves that he's a jerk and a clod, and he's arrogant, too! He thinks he's an Ivy-League world-class designer, and that I'm just a local hick who likes to play with a trowel every once in a while."

At this talk, Jade really got her game on and defended her home girl. "Girlfriend, you are Main Line gardening's finest designer, you've got it in your blood. I mean, you've been taking care of plants since birth;

didn't your dad give you a toy watering can when you were in the cradle? I mean, come on, who does he think he is?"

Isabella agreed, but she wanted to prove, without a shadow of a doubt, that she was the best landscape designer on the Main Line, college degree or not. She knew that her associate's degree was no match for his high-class background, but, she also was much savvier to the real-world demands of her clients. She built long-standing relationships with customers for whom she had executed their designs, and then helped set up a maintenance schedule for the properties through Albero Landscaping. Sure, Max's designs had more zing. Her work, however, held up to the test of time. In a year or two from now, his type of designs would leave the couple house poor from either outrageous maintenance costs, or the tedious job of replacing the plants that couldn't survive the oppressive heat or extreme cold of the area.

Jade said, "Maybe you could ask someone to judge your designs for all of these categories, like sustainability or affordable upkeep," Jade said, "Those Manicleer people would be great judges, since Jimmy's yard will be paying homage to their pleasure garden and all." Jade thought that this was getting fun, the idea of a gardening contest even had some entertainment value.

Isabella loved it when Jade got all cinematic and used words like "homage." Currently using her USC screenwriting degree to work in the Philadelphia film community, Jade really knew her stuff in that regard.

In fact, *thought* Jade silently, if the home improvement show got wind of this project, the viewers could be the ones to take a vote…she might know a person or two in Hollywood. Besides that, Isabella's personal life could use some shaking up; she's getting as cloistered as a hermit.

Isabella left the studio even more miffed than before. Even her best friend wasn't immune to the Max Ivy mystique.

Isabella decided to try again to get some friendly support for her kind of eco-friendly gardening. She drove over to Valley Forge Mountain using Route 23, a windy but fast road that was a good detour around the King of Prussia mall and its traffic nightmare. Her truck was getting pelted by the pouring rain. Well, I have driven in far worse weather, Isabella mused.

Once she shook off her raincoat and took off her shoes, she was lead to the kitchen in the large suburban home of her newest friend, Marissa. Isabella walked past some large windows with stunning views of the mountain, and was sorry that it was too rainy to take a walk a few miles away at Valley Forge National Park.

"So my dad was trying to protect me from being labeled as "the help" by the Mr. Ivy's of the world," she explained to her more plant-oriented, down-to-earth BFF, Marissa.

A few months ago, Marissa started working at the check-in desk at Manicleer, where Isabella met her while touring the grounds. They soon traded phone numbers and became good. Isabella was hoping for a plant-savvy point of view to get her through the project.

Marissa was busy in the kitchen, trying to learn how to cook Indian food so that she could surprise her husband with his childhood favorites. She had secured the recipes from her mother-in-law in Bangalore. The newly renovated, cherry-wood kitchen smelled like curry and other rich spices.

"So, you are saying that Max doesn't know that you were the live-in help? Well, I mean it was like the 80's and all, not the 30's or anything. How do you mean?" Marissa asked. Her blue eyes twinkled when a good story was in the wind.

Now that Marissa was finally expecting, she was trying to take it easy. While not entirely devoting herself to a strict confinement, she didn't want to tax her body. It had been such a blessing to finally get pregnant after so many years of tests and failed hopes.

"It was Mr. Ivy," Isabella explained, hoping that she would be offered some of the delicious-smelling Indian cuisine. "He was the type who told the live-in help that their children were not allowed to associate with his children, ride the bus together with them, or be in activities together."

"Well, for one thing, why did he send Max along to the same public school that y'all were going to, anyway, instead of an elite private school? Secondly, didn't you say you worked in a play together there?" Marissa asked. She was always wise to inconsistencies.

Isabella explained that in Lower Merion, the public schools were rated so highly that it was desirable for even the crème-de-la-crème to send their Harvard-bound there. She described her role behind the scenes on the stage crew for the musical, *Grease*, as having little to no contact with the cast. Max, however, had the starring role.

It was still mysterious to Marissa, the way that Main Liners seemed to cling to social strata for generations was the same way some people hold on to a good family recipe. Back in New England, where she was from, an oyster was an oyster, no matter what the package. Siddhartha, her husband of 5 years, had transferred here with his job at the green energy telecommunications company. Getting restless in her new town and wanting to meet people, she landed the job at Manicleer several years ago, where she was able to keep her plant roots tended. Plants were easy to understand. People, however, remained a mystery, especially those of the Main Line variety. The reasons behind their behaviors were often secretive.

She saw a need to break the silence, so she decided to parrot back what her friend had said. "So, you are sick of playing second fiddle to this guy, and want to show him that you are the plant mama in town."

Yes, that was pretty much it, Isabella agreed.

Isabella was pretty darned sick of being second fiddle to people like Mr. Max Ivy! Recalling a time when he won class president and she hadn't even been voted in as homeroom representative, she saddened. Sure, high school was a long time ago, and she realized she was holding onto her resentments a little too intensely. However, high school was just a taste of the whole Main Line experience. It wasn't just Max himself, but the type of privileged, and just plain lucky people that got her goat. Besides that, she really missed those ponies at the Ivy estate! To be thrown out of one's childhood home so abruptly was life altering.

Yes, Isabella was going to bring Max down a peg or two, she just wasn't quite sure how.

Chapter 8 - What on Earth?

"Annuals are like the costume jewelry of the plant world."
Real-life plant guru, Jerry Baker

Max returned from the stables exhilarated. It had been a long time since he had ridden Foxy, his amber mare. He had awakened to see the sunrise and to get some fresh air on his favorite path around the estate.

When Max returned to the main house, he was confused at the pile of banana peels deposited on the front step. "What on earth?" he questioned.

Left next to the tropical fruit carcasses was a tidy note that read, "This is for the planet, landscaper dude." It was signed, in messy and practically illegible penmanship, by a guy named Pete.

Oh, thought Max, Not another nutcase environmentalist. Whoever dropped this off is truly bananas! He had some contact initiated in Los Angeles by some of the granola eaters, but he had never been treated to banana peels. That was an original. Hopefully, he won't do it again. It wouldn't do for anyone to trip on a peel and sue him. Maybe that is what this about, thought Max, perhaps it is a scam.

Max disposed of the peels, but not the note (he would give it to Cyrus for investigation and storage). He entered the house and went directly to the breakfast room, where his mother, Camille, was sipping her tea.

Max's telephone rang, and he looked at the caller ID. It was his agent.

"Hey Max, I was out all night at a movie premier, it is five in the morning here. I never got any sleep, but I'm totally wired. My client was passing out these shooters that have the caffeine buzz. I'm home now, but had this incredible urge to talk on the phone, and I thought about the time zones. You are the only one I know who is currently on the east coast and who wakes up early. How are things going on your hiatus? Have you looked at the list of PR opportunities I faxed to you?"

"Yes, you do sound really hyper. Maybe you could use a good night's sleep." Max responded.

"Stop evading me. I own that maneuver, remember? You can't outmaneuver me! Now, back to the public relations blitz you are supposed to be doing?" Mindy Smart, his usually considerate agent, asked.

"No can do, this is strictly a vacation. I'm all about rest and relaxation, and I'm not going to stir up the fans any more than they already are."

"Sounds like you have encountered some loonies out east?" she asked.

"You wouldn't get people leaving banana peels if you went into a normal line of work," Camille said evenly, without even looking up from her morning repast.

Chapter 9 - Max Learns the Truth

"Give Me Park Avenue"
Green Acres theme song

Isabella woke up to the sound of the telephone; it was Jimmy. "Please don't be angry with me for calling so early on your day off," he said, "Yesterday was not a good day. I lost a lot in the stock market and my honeymoon budget looks like we're getting a free casino bus tour and complimentary buffet, if I'm lucky. We need to talk."

"What's to be angry about, it isn't my honeymoon," Isabella replied.

"Yeah, but now the budget for my garden is like nil. You are going to have to give me your other customer's weeds or something. I don't know, just make them pretty weeds because I want Lacey to come home from camp and be thrilled. She'll be there for the time when Char and I are on our honeymoon. Good thing the bride's side is paying for the rest of the to-do. Julia has hired a really great wedding planner, and things are going well, so I don't have to worry about any of that."

And worry he would, because Jimmy was a detail-oriented person on everything except when it came to fashion. He happily worked in the computer department of a major company, herding the other socially impaired, but appropriately attired employees to their fantasy football drafts and other indoor activities.

Truly, Isabella was bewildered when her nebbish-like cousin had caught the attention and won the heart of the fashion savvy and energetic socialite. Charlene was not only 12 years younger than Jimmy, but from a totally different social strata.

"Oh, and I totally forgot the reason I am calling you in the first place, Isabella. Charlene is begging me to ask your help with selecting the flowers at 'Hydrangeas and Tulips' this afternoon. She said she'll spring for dinner at your favorite restaurant if you help out," Jimmy said. "I told her you like simple meals, and not to go too fancy, by the way."

"See you at three o'clock," she sighed, "but don't worry about the landscaping budget. We get discounts on plant materials because we're in the trade, and my labor will be free. We'll use the free township compost. You'll see, it will all work out." Isabella reassured her cousin.

Charlene's uncle, Max, was also asked to meet at "Hydrangeas and Tulips" for the final floral consultation. The minute she saw him there, Isabella groaned. It was going to be so much harder to make intelligent bud selections. However, looking at the floral arrangements went better than Isabella expected. Well, she thought, there really isn't much to disagree on when it comes to a fall foliage theme. Months ago, Isabella had encouraged Charlene and Jimmy to try a sustainable pick-your-own flower garden in a rural area. Instead, Charlene had chosen this classy, but expensive, local florist. Despite this, they were able to choose a nice selection of locally grown flowers in all sorts of fall tones to offset the moss green-colored bridesmaid's gowns. The mothers of the bride and the flower girl, Lacey, were going to wear mint green. All in all, it was a very nice color palette, and also very simple. Thank goodness that they didn't want exotic, imported flowers; that would not be eco-friendly, she thought.

Isabella was relieved that the sleeveless bridesmaids' dress included a wrap. She knew she would feel self-conscious if she was really exposed. It was just she, Ruth Abrams, and an Ivy cousin in the bridal party, other than Charlene, of course. This was a nice, simple, and elegant way to keep things manageable, thought Isabella, who recalled a wedding of a second cousin, which included eight bridesmaids. That was on the Italian side of the family. She didn't have much contact with the Polish side, other than with Jimmy and his dad. So, it would be great to represent the Albero family at Jimmy's wedding. The flowers would also help her to hide a bit up there in front of all those people. She was looking forward to helping Jimmy and Charlene usher in their new life together and happy she could help in many little and big ways.

While Charlene certainly knew how to keep things simple, she also liked to go all-out when it came to fine dining. Leaving their own vehicles at the florist, they piled into Charlene's Lexus SUV to go to dinner. Max, Isabella, Jimmy, Charlene, Ruth, and Cyrus were on their way to a luxurious, five-star restaurant on the Main Line. Isabella thought that it was silly that they didn't just walk to the restaurant from the flower shop; it was only two blocks away. She did, however, enjoy all the extra legroom that the SUV had to offer, and she had a lot of leg to stretch out. That was one of her nicest attributes, and it was great that the bridesmaid's dress was going to cover much of her legs because it was tea-length. She was relieved that it wasn't too short, and was looking forward to the final fitting in a few weeks.

A premier world-renown chef named Françoise had extended his culinary expertise to the suburbs, and escorted their party personally to their table. Isabella, who realized that he was a local celebrity, was all smiles until they sat down to look at the menu. There was nothing on the menu that she pronounce, let alone wanted to eat. The only French food she liked was a croissant. The rest is icky snail food, or so she thought.

"Is everything okay?" Max whispered in her ear, as he noticed her face turning green.

Speaking in a soft voice directed at Max, she explained her situation. "French food really isn't my thing. The idea of heavy cream and snails, or anything French, sort of makes my stomach do cartwheels. Jimmy knew that it was the one cuisine that really repulsed me, but, he conveniently forgot when making these arrangements. Love does that to people; it gives them tunnel vision. Look at him, he's totally smitten."

Looking at the happy engaged couple, it was clear that Jimmy would go along with whatever Charlene wanted, anyway. Jimmy's complete attention was fixed on Charlene's happy glow, knowing that the florist was all wrapped up and ready. Charlene was relieved that she could enjoy her summer. If she ate in moderation and ran 15 miles a week, she could have her final fitting and still look stunning in her vintage Dior dress.

As Isabella frowned over the menu, Max leaned over, his strong thighs accidentally rubbing up against her. "I would suggest this salad here if you like tuna," Max said as he pointed to the item on the menu in her hands. "Perhaps you may want to consider some of these chicken dishes over here." He selected foods for her that were quite delectable, and Isabella started to see the lure of French cuisine.

The evening had really gone much better than Isabella expected, but it would clearly be impossible to get out of a second "double date" if she didn't come up with a plan.

After the surprisingly delicious dinner, Charlene, Jimmy, Isabella, Max, and a lurking Cyrus walked to downtown Wayne for dessert. While walking to the far end of town to check out the new coffee and ice cream bar, Isabella blurted out, "I've decided to join a convent." Gathering up courage, she said a bit louder, "I will probably go with the Grey Nuns. I really like what the Sisters of Charity do, but I really can't abide by their strict interpretation of the vow of poverty; it is too hard core for me. However, being in an order founded by the Blessed Mother Teresa of Calcutta is really enticing."

While Jimmy and Charlene made moon faces together, her cousin replied, "Sure, you've always talked about that; you'd be the gardening nun, kind of like the singing nun or flying nun or something," he said.

Max, who had never heard of such a plan, asked, "Is being on a date with me really souring you to all of this romantic companionship? Wow, that's quite a blow to my masculinity. I think I better watch a football game, drink beer, and get some swear words in just to feel better."

Isabella saw Cyrus smile out of the corner of her eye. She appraised the bodyguard and asked, "Is that what you and Cyrus do when you're not on the job?"

Max was not really eager to talk about himself or Cyrus, the brooding bodyguard, or really anything other than the lovely creature next to him, so he turned the topic to Isabella and her background.

"You know, earlier you mentioned that you went to Lower Merion. What year did you graduate?" Max asked.

As their conversation turned to their graduating year, it dawned on Max that he must have, at one point, seen her in the halls, the yearbook, or in the lunchroom.

"Did you look, well, remarkably different? Like, have you changed your appearance quite a bit? Why didn't I think to bring the old yearbook - that would settle this for good. It is killing me that I don't remember you."

Jimmy, overhearing everything, said, "You know, my cousin has always been really religious, kept a low profile, and just liked to observe other people."

As their party of six looked over and tasted a few of the ice cream selections, Isabella's curiosity got the best of her and she asked Max how he got into gardening.

"Well, years ago, I must have been 14 or so, we had in our employ a gardener who was just simply the best. He showed me how to take care of plants, how to really take care of anything, that's for sure. It was a rough time for me and, his name was Dan. He really got me thinking of how I could be not just a good gardener, but a better person.

Charlene, interrupting, said, "You are not going to believe this, but Isabella's dad is named Dan, and he's a gardener, and Jimmy, didn't you tell me he used to work at some of the big estates in the area?"

"My grandfather was your grandfather's gardener, and my dad served your father in that capacity as well, until 1992 or so." Isabella explained.

"Isabella, are you serious? I never put two and two together. I can't believe I didn't know that Uncle Dan was Charlene's grandfather's gardener. Char, this is so great, it is another connection between us. It is like kismet or something." Jimmy gushed.

"I will never forget Gardener Dan, he was my first and very best mentor," Max said in a gentle tone. "My folks were applying the usual pressure to follow in Dad's footsteps; Ivy League, grad school, and then get into a very high-paying line of work. My dad made it quite clear that the idea of studying landscape design was totally forbidden. But, I did it anyway, and he never knew about it until I started on the *Homes on the Move* program. I had to triple major in Economics, Foreign Policy, and Landscape Design. It was a rigorous line of study and required five years, but the rowing scholarship I got kept me in demand at the college. They also gave me a teaching subsidy to serve as an assistant teacher for some of the freshman classes. My parents knew only that I was studying to be a diplomat or a senator, and that the rowing coach liked having me around."

Isabella was impressed with Max's scholarly devotion to their mutual craft, and his high regard for her father. But, she still kept wondering about the ripped out plants that she saw strewn all over Dan's shed. She made a mental note to ask him about that later, sometime when they could talk in a more private location. The idea of being in a secluded spot with Max, instead of repulsing her, now made her tingle and shiver all over. This was a new and welcome sensation, and it felt very right.

"Well, here my parents were, during my college years, bragging about their son, the future business man, diplomat or whatever, and here I was, trying to figure out how to get a gig working outside under the big sky and taking care of the plants the way my pal Dan had taught me. Truthfully, he was the only person who ever really gave a crap about what I wanted out of life, and didn't just want me to be what they wanted me to be."

"Sir, if I may ask," Cyrus pried, "how could such a lovely young lady evade your radar, if, let's say, she was living in your gatehouse for your entire youth?"

"Cyrus is asking, how could I be so invisible?" Isabella's sense of justice was piqued. "That's a good question. Back then, 'the help' used back entrances, didn't spend time with the family, kept to ourselves or risk getting kicked out. But, in our case, we got kicked out even though we followed every rule."

"Ironically, however, my dad never held it against any of you. And Max, you were one of his favorites. My dad always did say nice things about you, and at graduation and the school play he was sure to see what you were up to," said Isabella.

At this revelation, Max's ears perked up, sort of like a border collie. A new light came into his eyes, and he was more curious than ever.

"You know, come to think of it, I always did sort of think I saw him at those events, but I thought it was just wishful thinking. I mean, why would a former gardener be coming to see me?" There was a gentle hitch in Max's voice, and for a few minutes, he was not the international playboy, or the grown-up Main Line aristocrat, but, merely, a boy who missed his favorite mentor.

Trying to get the conversation a tad lighter, Jimmy mentioned that it was the first time that he'd seen his cousin enjoy French cuisine, and he thanked Max for helping his cousin with the menu. To that, Max replied, "It was my pleasure. Did you know that the American, Julia Child, was the first to write an English language cookbook of French food? And, Julia was in the diplomatic corps."

"Was she a master spy and a master chef?" Charlene asked.

Isabella, who was happy to change the subject, said, "No, she was just a typist at the state department, her husband was a diplomat, and she had free time and wanted to learn how to cook in France. She fell in love with that cuisine and lifestyle and wanted to share it with her countrymen."

Max said, "So, she was able to pursue her dreams, find herself, still be married, and in love. No need to join the chaste nuns of whatever, Isabella."

That's when it hit him, the name Isabella. An echo of a childhood taunt, "Izzie, Izzie rhymes with dizzy," rang in his head…

She was *that* Isabella. The overly serious one with the big tortoise-shell glasses, which hid her almond-shaped eyes, porcelain skin, and just about her whole face. Young Isabella's hair was in an unfashionable hairdo, and frequently in braids. She was that urchin who lived near the train station. He cringed; he was the bane of her existence.

"Weeds are the bane of my existence," she said, as if reading his mind, as if he were a weed. "My dad taught me some really nontoxic ways to clear out the brush on a new site, so we aren't just sharing space with the weeds, you know, cohabitating."

At the sound of the word, "cohabitation," images of a scantily clad and fully toned female gardener lying on his bed flooded his mind. However, the woman in front of him was fully dressed, and fully serious. She probably was so uptight she wouldn't even kiss a man on a first date, let alone someone who had been so rude to her back in school.

He recalled that when she was crossing past his friends at the train station, they would tease her mercilessly. She was just so cute being a teenager and wearing braids, they called her "Miz Izzie" because she held her head up high and was sort of above everyone. Looking back, she might not have enjoyed the taunting.

Memories of his youth filtered through to his consciousness. Come to think of it, he thought, maybe he had seen her at the estate a few times. So, she was Dan's daughter. That would explain why she was so passionate about gardening.

"You know, the Ivy estate has never been quite as beautiful since your dad left the scene. He left so suddenly." Max was really heartbroken when he learned that Dan was going to be leaving and that he wasn't going to be able to say goodbye. He went to the shed to find him, but was told that Dan had already left the estate, for good. No reason was given, and it was one of the most disappointing times in his life.

"Well, he didn't want to go, or anything, but they didn't give him a choice," she confided, sadly.

"Who didn't give him a choice, his new business partners?" Max asked, suddenly curious, as someone gets when a decades-old mystery is about to be solved.

She looked at him, directly, and said, "Your dad kicked us off the land, said it was time to go and to not come back. Then he accused my dad of stealing $500, which my dad would never do."

At the word of $500, Max was shocked! He vaguely recalled something about missing money back then, but he couldn't put it all together and his head was spinning.

"If you don't mind, I'd like to head home. It has been a delightful afternoon and evening, and I need to get some rest. Thank you, Charlene and Jimmy, for your hospitality. I'll walk back to my car." Max hastily excused himself from the gathering, hoping to go home to get some answers from his parents.

Chapter 10 - Prune, Plant, or Pilfer?

"There was no missing $500."
Camille to her son, Max

When Max returned home, he immediately summoned his mother, who had been expecting this interrogation since she had heard that the gardeners pretty, little girl was now in the scene. She wasn't relishing the opportunity to describe her character flaws and mistakes from the past, but, in some ways it was a relief to finally confess.

"There was no missing $500, it was not like that," said a remorseful Camille Ivy to her son, Max.

"What are you telling me, Mother?" Max asked in a weary tone of voice. He was already feeling like a heel for having made someone, especially someone so lovely, feel invisible. The last thing he wanted was for his family to have played a part in a sad chapter in Isabella's life.

"I am positive, Max, dear," Camille began her explanation, "that with time and careful thought you would understand and forgive me. I was finding myself shopping more and more, with all of the functions that we are expected to attend. The saleswomen would call me up to share the latest on an unadvertised sale, and she had a dress that was just my size," explained Camille.

"It wasn't an addiction, or anything. I just had to maintain a certain standard in my apparel. Really, spending $500 wasn't a great deal of money at all, for a dress to attend the sort of functions that Main Line families like us are pressed into attending," said Camille. "There are always so many charitable events and fundraisers, you wouldn't even believe it. The point is that my credit card bill was in the tens of thousands, and I didn't want to max it out, so I took the cash from your father's drawer without mentioning it him."

By the time she heard of the gardener's dismissal, it was really too late to set everything straight. She just allowed the misunderstanding, and was sure to pass on some good words of recommendation to her friends who may need landscaping work. They understood about the shopping, it was something that was routinely done. "I thought it was for the best," said Mrs. Ivy, "and I never expected it to bite me in the back in this way."

"Well, Mother, I guess you aren't the only one that has to make amends to the Albero family," responded a crestfallen Max. Perhaps, he thought, by making a terrific garden for Jimmy and Charlene, we can put this all in the past. All it will take is for me to work peacefully with Isabella, and how difficult can that be?

As Camille and Max, fully reliving the errors of the past, were reduced to fitful slumbers in their different bedchambers, Rochelle slept like a baby.

While her clueless husband slept, she was tying up the last details to make a seamless flight to the Cayman Islands. All the physical training and Botox was making her more attractive, but she still just felt like helpless Regina. The offshore cosmetic surgery would allow her to become the kind of classy broad that would attract to her all kinds of opportunities. In just two days, she would be able to begin her new life.

That night, Max tossed and turned in a deep slumber. It was a typical humid summer evening, the type of weather when at any time, a storm may break.

He was having a packed lunch in a wicker basket filled with cheese and crackers and fresh fruit. They sat down at the most remote picnic table at Valley Forge National Park. Her long skirt bundled up around her legs. The lady, brunette with long, luscious wavy hair and cherry red lips, was dressed in old fashioned, elegant clothing. They were eating cherries and joking about how they should have brought an umbrella. The sky was rapidly darkening; climate could be so changeable in July.

Just as she got up to see a deer off in the distance, she tripped on some equipment left over from some previous campers. He joked that if it rained, he would have to walk her back to the awaiting car. All of a sudden, rain started teeming down.

Max swooped in and snuggled the lovely lady in his arms, carrying her to safety.

He awoke alone, to the rising sun and drenched in sweat, with one name on his lips, "Isabella."

Chapter 11 - Breakfast of Champions

"We named him Maximilian because he'll make a million."
Harrison Alexander Ivy to his father, Spencer, upon the birth of his son

The Ivy's idea of a simple family brunch would appear extravagant to some. To celebrate Max's visit home, Camille instructed Cook to create a salmon pate and cold vegetable tray with assorted quiches and crepes.

The family was slowly trickling into the breakfast room when Harrison Alexander Ivy entered with a loud, "Maximilian, it's good to see you. Have you made your first million yet?"

He vigorously shook his son's hand.

"Uh, hi Dad, I'm on the phone with my agent, I'll be with you shortly." Max cringed at the unintended pun.

"Make it snappy. In my day, you wouldn't dare talk on the phone at a meal," Mr. Ivy commanded. "I guess the girls are busy with wedding planning, so we have you all to ourselves right now."

Mindy, his agent, had attended a movie premier with some of her clients the previous night. The partying had continued until the wee hours of the morning, capped off with some caffeine-loaded alcohol-based shooters. While New York is the city that doesn't sleep, it was from Los Angeles that Max's agent called. She had not yet gone to sleep, and desperately wanted to get some projects going.

Mindy continued, "Through an East Coast contact, I've gotten wind of this dueling gardener thing you have going with the sexy brunette. I hear there's amazing, hot, sexy chemistry and I'm seeing lots of possibilities here. The reality TV market is always looking for fresh blood."

"No, I'm not interested," said Max, quite bluntly. "Thanks, though. And, please do not take this project idea beyond this phone conversation."

"The heck I'm not!" replied the wound-up-tight agent with a killer buzz. "We're talking big ratings, big exposure, and..." Max knew what was coming next, "big bucks!"

"Unless the program you have in mind is rated G for green, this girl will not be interested. She is only about the environment. We're not an item, and she's practically a nun. Please, just leave it alone," pleaded Max.

Realizing that she was not making any headway, Mindy decided to backpedal a little. "Well I am sorry to hear you aren't interested. If you change your mind, that nun angle has some possibilities," Mindy plead.

"Oh, and speaking of the environment, what's with the banana peels? I agreed to open your packages when it was panties, because that was fun and I could soak them in Clorox and give them a good machine wash, and add them to my thong collection. These banana peels, I've got to say, are slime city. We had enough to start a compost pile. Oh, I've go to go, the caffeine is wearing off and I'm about to crash."

"Goodbye to you, too," Max deadpanned.

"Well, Dad, I'm all yours," Max said, turning to his father.

"Max, I'm glad to hear that there is nothing going on with that Isabella woman," his father said.

"And this would be because?" questioned an angry Max.

"We've agreed to allow Charlene to marry down. She was going with that rough crowd for a while, you remember, the party-hearty crowd. We were worried she would end up on drugs or covered in tattoos. The day she met James at the Phillies game was a miracle. He is a nice, clean young man. She can help raise his daughter and give her a stable home. By the time Lacey is a busy teen, or in college, Charlene will be ready to find a more appropriate husband."

"Your father is saying that this is Charlene's starter marriage, Max. Everybody knows that," said a quiet and reserved Camille.

"Yes, and so, it is incumbent that you are seen with people that are in our social sphere. We are not going to lose everything that we have gained in all these centuries in America by becoming just like everyone else," Mr. Ivy insisted. "That's not how we raised you, Max. You are trained to be the best, and you should associate with only the best."

"I will be seen with Isabella, or whomever else I might choose to associate with, regardless of their *standing* in society," said Max. He was secretly imagining Isabella standing while wearing one of his shirts, and nothing else.

"Well, don't be surprised if she's after your money," retorted his father. "She might try to trick you into getting her pregnant. Just never believe a girl when she says that she has everything taken care of and not to worry."

"Listen to your father about being protected, Max. There are all kinds of disease out there," said Camille. "Even a nice girl could have one," she added, so as not to seem overly harsh about Isabella.

"She's not that kind of girl, I'll have you know. She's…" Max searched for the right words to describe Isabella's sweetness. "She's pure. She is not trying to do anything here but plan a garden and make sure it is sustainable with low upkeep."

At this point, Charlene, and her mother, Julia, walked quietly into the room. They had just met with the large-lipped wedding planner, Rochelle, at her office. It seemed like a nice idea to stop by the main house to see if Max was around. He was everybody's favorite in the family, and they all had great expectations for him.

Having absorbed the significant points from the conversation from where she had been perched outside the breakfast room door, Charlene was ready to share her opinion.

"Isabella? Shut up! I knew you were getting cozy, that's awesome." She said, very enthusiastically, "I've been trying to get you two together! You are, like, made for each other."

Charlene was twenty-three going on sixteen as she described this very romantic pairing using a schoolgirl vocabulary and inflection.

"Sorry to burst your bubble, but Isabella is not interested in me. I am not her type; she's joining a convent or something," said a newly shy Max.

"Oh, that's hogwash. Jimmy said she started talking about becoming a nun after her fiancé, Robby Sabatini, the carpenter, broke her heart." Charlene said, as she tasted the crudités.

Max was surprised to hear of a failed engagement in Isabella's past. He had imagined that he was the only man to ever hold her tightly, even if it was during a kitchen snafu. He started to feel a pang of annoyance that someone else had been intimate with her. Unused to feeling jealousy, he brushed off the feeling with a shrug. Well, the idea that a girl in this day and age could actually be a virgin was pretty ridiculous. Of course, she had been engaged. What man wouldn't want her to be his?

"Oh, that reminds me, I'll stay around this week so we can have a nice visit and then I'd like to have use of the shore house the following week." Max asked.

"Sure Max, and invite whomever you want," said a defiant Camille, giving her son a subtle wink.

"Ah, Mom," interjected an annoyed Julia Ivy, Charlene's socialite mother. "That isn't fair. You promised the shore house to me and my friends next week. Remember, my MOB sobfest? My friends have all made arrangements with their husbands, bosses, or babysitters to be able to take a few days to help me get my groove back.

The cheerleaders, thought Max, when he heard about the clique of friends that Julia kept in touch with through thick and thin. Their cheering moves had made quite an impression on him in his youth, but the moniker, while accurate, did not fully describe the very essence of this group. They were simply "the best" that the Lower Merion class of '82 had to offer. Lower Merion Cheerleaders were not just attractive, thin, and energetic. They were also all-star students, athletically superior, the cool kids, and always had the best clothes and the best boyfriends. While the group was an eclectic mix of ethnicities, they all had one thing in common. They could stand for nothing less than the best in themselves and others.

Sophie was an accomplished muralist and part-time fundraiser for the Philadelphia Museum of Art. In high school, she had been both a cheerleader and an artist, which was an unusual combination. Currently, her daughter, Ruth, ran a successful catering company on the Main Line. The other former cheerleaders were mostly professionals, doctors, and lawyers, married to professionals, or divorced from professionals. It was hard for Max to keep track.

"Well, that shouldn't be a problem, kids. That house was built to accommodate several families. We used to have the Abrams family visit all the time. There's plenty of space. Why Max, you could even allow Cyrus a guest, maybe he has a special someone to bring along."

"No way," said a loyal Julia, "Sophie would shoot me if we encouraged competition! Ruth has had her eyes on Cyrus."

"Ruth is going, too, Julia?" Camille asked.

"Well of course, who do you think is going to be preparing our meals for us? We don't cook!"

"Well, that's brilliant, come to think of it. Everyone should have friends who are caterers!" replied an encouraging Camille.

"Make sure she asks for the family discount at the grocery there when she goes for supplies," insisted a shrewd and frugal Mr. Harrison

Alexander Ivy. "Cook can fill her in on the right markets to go to, have her give him a call."

Max was thinking about how frugal his father could be, but that was common amongst the wealthiest gentry of the fabled Main Line. "How do you think we got this way?" was a phrase repeated in his youth when he dared to question this philosophy.

"Julia, you called it a 'sobfest', what's that about? What on earth is an MOB? Is this some sort of plastic surgery?" Max asked.

Julia was silent, and a bit sullen.

"Sister might be a bit under duress over her status as an almost mother of the bride, which is a step from," Camille said softly, pausing for effect, "grandmother-hood, which has got her on a low. But her girls, those cheerleaders, they'll pull her through. They always do."

Chapter 12 - Road Trip

"Nothing in life is free."
Camille's mother to her grandchildren, Max and Julia

Isabella was planning to drive her own truck, but it needed last-minute repairs. She didn't like to rely on others unless she had to. She talked about skipping the needed mechanical work, but Dan didn't like his daughter to be driving an unreliable vehicle across the state. He insisted that she ride over with Max, offering her a ride to the Ivy estate so that her car could be in the shop for the much-needed servicing.

Dan dropped her off in front of the main gate, not wanting to chase ghosts by entering the Ivy compound. There were so many memories, good and bad; he would leave that for another day.

Max said he would be taking the Land Cruiser, which sounded like a good, reliable car to Isabella.

As he pulled out of the enclosed garage, however, she saw that the vehicle was vintage 1972. She didn't even know that Toyotas were made back then. In addition, it was bright green and missing some conspicuous pieces.

"Max, where are the doors to the Land Cruiser?" Isabella asked in disbelief.

"They're in the back, but I'll put them on if the weather changes. I like to ride like this in the summer, it is all fresh air, I'm telling you. You'll love it, Isabella!" Max said slyly, "Plus, it's green, and I'm a great driver!"

Max was driving the vintage, beat-up, sporty vehicle because it exuded a certain laid-back charm. Plus, it really drove his father to the brink. It was completely inappropriate for someone of his lineage and social standing, according to the stodgy Mr. Harrison Alexander Ivy, to be driving such a pile of crap.

As they drove through the Main Line into Center City, Philadelphia, Isabella noticed a few creative driving moves. His sporadic driving implied distaste for the rules of the road and a devil-may-care attitude.

Isabella, who was totally windblown and flabbergasted by this point, calmly said, "Where did you get your driver's license, by mail order?"

Max promised to be more cautious, and did slow down a bit, so they were able to have a more relaxed conversation. Now she didn't have to zing him about his driving.

As Max drove over the Ben Franklin Bridge and into New Jersey, Isabella shouted out some of her early preparation for the garden redo.

"I'm having the crew revitalize the yard and eliminate the weeds with geosulfate, as it is less toxic than the chemical herbicide alternatives. I think that it won't spoil the surprise if we find out from Charlene what her favorite color for mulch is; she knows that I am doing a few minor alterations." Isabella took out her cell phone, "I'll send her a text."

"Yes, do that when you're not driving, I'm giving you the controls," Max said.

Max slowed down on a main thoroughfare in Camden, and took a few turns off the highway to slower streets to switch drivers. He stopped the Land Cruiser with a flourish, and, indicated that he was ready for Isabella to assume the driver's role.

"Here?" She asked, as she realized that they were in an area that was probably zone zero for drug and gang activity during the later hours of the day.

"I think I have a cramp in my leg, it is your turn to drive. Let's switch places," Max said in a very controlled, calm voice.

After rapidly switching seats, Isabella sat low in the driver's seat and looked at the controls. "Do you always allow the gas to get so low?"

Cyrus, driving an army issue Humvee, drove up with replacement gas and a stern look.

"It happens every time, Boss. You always go for the less expensive fuel in New Jersey, and then you run out."

"Fellas," said Isabella, "I think we're getting a lot of attention here, can we just get back on the road?"

Going over the bridges into Long Beach Island, Max asked, "Isabella, may I ask, what are your thoughts on James and Charlene, I mean, as a couple?"

"Yeah, they're a couple alright," she giggled, "a couple of nutcases..." Then she got serious. "Well, Jimmy is very happy with Charlene, they are like two peas in a pod. But, well, he's not very stylish, you know, he's comfortable, financially speaking, but not rich. I don't really see how it is going to work. But, hopefully it will all work out and it won't be a total disaster. And, if it all falls through, well, I hope they stay amicable, for Lacey's sake, at least."

"So, to summarize, you think it is Charlene's starter marriage?" he asked.

Her silence evaded a response.

Max made a few turns once on the island and ended up in North Beach. As Isabella saw the huge, white-columned home, Max explained how the island is long and narrow, and that the bay is on one side and the ocean is on the other.

She laughed, "Yeah, I know that, I've been coming here with my grandparents since I was a child. Uncle Johnny had a house in Beach Haven, near the pier."

They arrived at the shore house and Cyrus offered to take their bags up to the residence areas. This left Isabella and Max with time to spend out on the beach. There was a nice sea breeze, and it was heavenly.

Isabella offered to help Max water the attractive foundation plantings, and they ended up pruning and deadheading the hydrangeas. She saw the tender way he nurtured, and said, "Why did you do it?"

"What?" he asked.

"Rip out the house plant. It was magnificent one minute and then torn down and strewn all over the shed like a murder victim."

Max stopped what he was doing and rubbed the sweat off his brow with the back of his gloved hand. "It was a rough time. I wanted to enter some juried exhibitions at the art center, and my father forbade it. I felt like I was missing out on so much, just sort of feeling impoverished, so I went into the brandy in Dad's office."

"I thought that was just in the movies that rich people had decanters of brandy in their drawing rooms," she said.

"You don't understand, your dad wanted you to be your own person, to stay true to yourself," Max said in a defensive tone.

"Yeah, but how can you be complaining about your upbringing?" Isabella argued. "You got everything you ever wanted."

"I'm not going to apologize for coming from a wealthy family. There are things my parents have done for me that are amazing, such as first class educational and travel opportunities. But," Max said slowly, for emphasis, "no, I did not get everything that I ever wanted. There's a price for privilege, and that is expectations which become limitations. Nothing in life is free, is what my grandmother used to always say."

"It's funny, though," Isabella said, "Your grandmother's gardener was my grandfather, and your grandmother's cook, you know about that right?"

"Let me guess," said Max. "She was your grandmother?"

"No way, my grandmother was a librarian. I got you!" She tussled his hair and did a "tag" move and he chased her playfully around to the other side of the house.

Isabella almost ran into a rusted metal sign with weeds growing over it. She brushed off the front of the sign, and it read, "For Sale."

Max asked if she was all right, and if she had any cuts or bruises from running into the sign. She said she didn't, but that her tetanus shots were up to date.

He explained the sign with a dismissive, "Oh, that. My father has had it in his head that we should put the house up on the market asking a total fortune. Nobody in their right mind would ever pay his asking price, so it has been listed for years. I don't think anyone has ever been interested, especially in this economy."

Isabella quietly wondered what the asking price for this sort of dwelling would be, but decided that it didn't matter, and dropped the subject.

They completed the gardening chores and washed up at an outdoor hosing station. They dried off with fluffy towels that were left on the line to dry. Isabella thought that the line added a sweet, homey touch and appreciated the Ivy's use of the soft sea breeze to dry the towels.

Max showed Isabella to a room he felt would be to her liking. It had a garden view on one side and a beach view from the other side. After they both had a chance to freshen up, he took her on a brief tour of the beach home. Isabella was astounded by the Great Room, which had views of the bay from one side and the beach from the other side.

Ruth had prepared a light brunch of pasta salad with capers and a fruit tray, which the cheerleaders were enjoying in the dining room. Max beckoned Isabella, holding two filled-up plates for each of them, into the kitchen, one of his favorite rooms.

They constructed their plans for the next few days. Mornings would be for relaxing and enjoying the beachside community, and afternoons would be for working on the garden plans. Then in the evening, they would have a light dinner and find some entertainment to cap off the day. It was easy to strike up a schedule, and it looked to be a relaxed way to complete the planning portion of the project.

It was decided that the study, which was on the bay-view side of the home, would be their creative station. It took a few hours to get into the groove of the project. Isabella was adamant that they forgo any and all over-the-top creative expressions, and keep the project simple. She also insisted on local, native, sustainable plants and materials, and recycling previously used supplies whenever possible.

Max felt that if they simplified things too much, it would lack any sort of zing, and would be a dreary, yawn-inducing garden fiasco.

They worked on the garden plans for several hours, trying to make concessions and compromises whenever possible. Needing a break, Max asked Isabella if she wanted to see the billiards room, as he had neglected to include that in the cursory tour.

The octagonal-shaped small room included a window-lined alcove with a bay view. Since the sun set on the bay, this was an ideal place to spend an evening. Right then, the sun was still shining bright, as it was only one in the afternoon, and the pool table beckoned.

"Oh, and these are the cues. Here's how to put the blue chalk on them, it helps with the friction." Max conducted a tour of the billiards room in a sultry, seductive way, as this had worked for him with the women in his past.

"And, here are the balls, which are stacked just so. How about a game, Isabella?" he drawled.

"I'll play," she replied, "but since I am so grateful to you for this great tour of your lovely home, let's put a wager on this game. How about, if you win, we do the garden project your way?"

"Sure," said Max, "I'm always up for a challenge."

As she started setting up the pool table, it became obvious to anybody but a trained seal, that she was an experienced pool player. When she made her first three shots and had almost cleared the table, Max could clearly see who was being played.

"OK, so I am going to go out on a limb and say that you have played pool before," he said.

"I learned from some of Manyunk's finest," Isabella said, as she thought about her former finance, Robby Sabatini. They would meet after work and shoot some pool, hang out in her neighborhood or his, and have a lot of fun. That was before she realized that all men, even Robby, were just after one thing, and one thing only, and it wasn't to play pool.

Her years with Robby had taught her many lessons, and how to play pool was just the half of it. Right now, though, she was benefiting from the patience he had shown her as he taught her how to handle her pool cue. As she sent all the balls, including the black one, into the corner pockets, she put up her hand for a high five. She turned to Max, expecting a buddy salute.

Instead of giving her a high-five, Max took her hand and used his considerable strength to pull her to him. As her body melted into his, she looked up to his face and saw a big smile.

"Isabella, for such a sweet girl, that was a very, very bad thing to do. You swindled me. I think you owe me a kiss to make up for it," cajoled Max in a seductive voice. And, without giving her much time to think about the ramifications of said kiss, he swooped in, planting a big one on her lips. He held her in a comforting embrace, and kissed her softly.

After they came up for some fresh air, the room was uncomfortably quiet. "How come a good catch like you is still single?" Max just sort of blurted out to diffuse the tension.

"Well, I was engaged, but it didn't work out," Isabella explained. "Robby and I had a major disagreement about the meaning of the word…" As Isabella was about to explain what finally broke apart her engagement to the young man that everyone in her life said was made for her, Max's cell phone buzzed.

He stood up at the sound of the phone, and when he saw it was Charlene, he put it on speaker, thinking that Isabella would want to hear what the bubbly redhead had to say.

"Good, I got you, Max, well, I'm so annoyed that everyone says this marriage is a starter marriage, I mean, I'm all-in, and so is Jimmy, you know. Oh, and don't even get me started about Grandfather. I've been working so hard to get you & Isabella together, you know I'm a born romantic, and, anyway, what a snob! I'm not to even mention that you and Isabella are dating. Can you imagine? Grandmother Camille says that it would make Grandfather apoplectic. By the way, what do you think about party favors, what about truffles…?"

As Charlene droned on about the wedding details, Isabella started to put the pool table back together. She was insulted and hurt by Camille's snub, and again, felt belittled and invisible. That was when she glanced down at the ground and saw a crumpled up piece of paper that looked like it had fallen out of Max's pocket.

She was going to respect his privacy and leave it alone, until she saw her name.

The note was in a fancy penmanship and said, "Dear Max: I forgot to tell you the numerical combination to the wall safe. It is 29349; I suggest you put your cash and valuables in there with that Albero woman around. I know her kind, always hanging around. This one may be playing hard to get, but there's no way she's as innocent as you say. If she's anything like her mother, who was a party girl in New York in the 70's, you need to keep your cash in the safe. I've heard from sources that she was after Alistair Ames and his fortune until he caught on. I don't want you leg-shackled to a loser like my brother is, all because he couldn't keep his pants up. I know I haven't always shown you my interest, but I do care about you and have always had your best interest at heart." It was signed, "Father."

Max saw Isabella with a crestfallen expression, reading the note that he had formerly crumpled up and put in his pocket. He had every intention of discreetly throwing the note in a lit fireplace, or a nifty shredder, or the bottom of a landfill, which was where it belonged. He never expected it to fall out and cause a problem. His father's advice was a bunch of garbage! He knew to pay no heed to his father's warnings; it was a snobbery issue, plain and simple. Now, his father was meddling in his personal life. This had to stop. Max called out, "Wait, Isabella, we need to talk!" But, quickly and quietly, she fled the room in tears.

Once up to her room, she curled up in fetal position on the bed, her cheeks stained with tears. She had to get a grip on her emotions. Panic set in, and then she fumbled for her cellular phone and dialed Jade's phone number.

"I'm driving back from Philly; we were down at a club for the wrap-up party for the cast, glad to be done with that one. What's up, Isabella? Jade asked. "Is it Max? Is he still a dunderhead like he was in high school?"

Priscilla sighed, and then said, "He's a member of the Ivy family. What do you expect? They think they are better than everyone else."

Isabella described the hostile, negative, slanderous descriptions of her and her mother given to Max from his father as a warning. "Get this, he told Max to put his cash in the safe with an Albero woman around."

"And did he?" Jade asked.

"I doubt it. I'm sure Max knows what his dad is up to," said Isabella.

"Isabella, those people are snobs," Jade said. "It doesn't mean that Max feels that way. He is smart enough to realize a total lie. Really, making up stories about the dead, it is unconscionable! I am going to turn this car around and head back east! I don't like you being this upset out there away from home. Didn't Max say that you could bring guests, anyone at all, down to the shore?"

"Yeah, but he was probably hoping I'd bring my dad. You know, for old times and all."

"Well, you need some reinforcements; I'm driving down there. Guess I should go home and pack my bags first, and make a plan on how to get back at those snotty "Poison Ivy" weeds. I'll be knocking at the door first thing in the morning, and I'm going to make Max carry my bags up those steps. Let those Ivys get a taste of their own medicine! How dare they act all snobby about you and make up lies about your dear mother, Sharon Rose - we'll just out-snob them and out-maneuver them. What about Marissa? I could drive her there, too, and the two of us will have Max Ivy wishing he never was born with that silver spoon in his mouth!"

"I couldn't ask her to do that, Marissa needs to rest," Isabella said.

"Isabella, Marissa is expecting, not incapacitated. We'll pull up a lawn chair for her the minute we get down there. Oh, and Isabella, be sure to wear the sunscreen, loads of it."

That evening, Isabella took her dinner out to the beach and went to bed at eight. The insult on herself and her mother, of all people, kept her from having a restful sleep.

Chapter 13 - One-upping the Ivys

"Revenge is best served cold."
Camille Ivy to her daughter, Julia, and son, Max

The maid's buzzer sounded at least 20 times, waking a rumpled, sleep-tossed Max from his bed. Harrison had installed the buzzer system at the beach house compound so that his wife's every need could be taken care of by the household staff, leaving him off the hook. He liked to sleep in, so it was especially useful in the morning. However, the Ivy staff was currently at the Main Line estate. So, Max followed in his father's footsteps, and paid Cyrus well to take care of menial tasks to free his time for more prurient interests.

"What in the blazes?!" Max muttered, as he hopped out of bed in his boxers. Quickly locating a pair of shorts, he didn't have time to comb down his sandy colored hair, so it was sticking up in all directions. "Why isn't anyone getting that buzzer?"

"Where's Cyrus?" he bellowed from the top of the stairs.

Isabella walked up the winding stairs to face her adversary. "He's indisposed; he took the morning off to go with Ruth to the market. But, fear not, Ruth has left out a cold breakfast buffet in the sitting room, so nobody is to starve. Well, except for you. You have work to do, no time for dilly-dallying. Now, Max, there are some important people parked on the driveway, and I need you to take care of their bags and make them comfortable."

Max was very confused. Isabella, his guest, was ordering him around and treating him like he was her servant.

Just as they both managed to squeeze down the circular steps to the bottom level, he saw the glint in her eyes. She was up to something. Serves me right, he thought to himself, for having a parent as ruthless as Harrison Alexander Ivy.
So, this is Isabella's type of revenge for his father treating her like dirt. Well, Max thought, I guess I can take it if she can dish it out, she'll get

it out of her system. How bad can it be? What will she have me do next, dig trenches?

Max soon found out how challenging his assignment would be when a harsh honking noise was heard outside, emanating from the driveway. Max was recoiling from the noises, as he headed towards the dining room, where a magnificent spread of pastries, muffins, and bagels awaited, but not for him. The honking continued. And then, he saw that his quiet beachside retreat was being descended on by…a gaggle of giggling garden girls.

Jade walked in and said, "Oh Max, dear, please get off of your lazy, indolent, aristocratic butt and carry some of these bags inside!"

A very pregnant brunette with no visible body fat, but a rounded belly bump swung open the front door. When she saw Max, she demanded, "We are having my baby shower next week and we need time to plan. Can you please take these bags upstairs and leave us alone with the pastries?"

"Yes, Max, aren't you going to show us to the sitting room?" Jade asked.

Max dutifully directed the ladies to the living room, but he was beginning to realize that he was going to be surrounded by hostile, demanding women on what was supposed to be the most relaxing part of his hiatus. This cold treatment was definitely all because of the letter that his father wrote.

Once there, Marissa plopped down on the big, cushiony sofa, took a sip from her water bottle and started to chat with the ladies. Max went to take the bags upstairs, but first he took a look at just how pregnant this Marissa woman appeared.

Watching Max eying her protruding stomach, Marissa explained, "I know, I know…I'm very, very pregnant. My husband, Sid, is on a business trip, and I didn't want to be alone. I was so happy to get Isabella's call, and Sid is thrilled that I'll be well taken care of. Don't get me wrong, at first he was worried, he gets so overprotective. But he went online and checked out the closest hospital, Atlantic, and they have an excellent rating. The local EMTs have a good reputation, and, besides, I told him, right on the beach I'll find most of the obstetricians in the tri-state area getting their tan on. In fact, my favorite doctor from my practice is out on vacation this week. I wouldn't be surprised if she is out here getting her tan on, too! Oh, I feel like a cow, but I feel great. Doctor says I've got to stay hydrated, though!"

"I've heard Cyrus is great at martial arts, so I'm hoping he'll show me a move or two," Jade commented.

"Ahem!" Max, covered head to toe in luggage, cleared his throat from the hallway. "There seems to be quite a large number of suitcases; is anybody running away from home?"

"These black bags are for Isabella; please place them gently in her room," said Marissa. Looking back at the girls, she said, "The extra bags are full of summer clothes that I have outgrown," as she looked down at her stomach and winced.

Jade said, "I was stunned when you told me about how old-fashioned your husband is. I can't believe he is saying that a new mother shouldn't wear sexy clothes."

"Yeah, he wants me to dress more conservatively, now that I'm going to be a mom, but I don't blame him, it is his culture. He comes from a very traditional background. He wants me to have a whole new wardrobe," explained Marissa. "I'm not going to turn down a chance to shop, but, these sundresses and other stuff are so cute, they shouldn't go to waste."

Jade opened up a bag, and a revealing chemise came out. Everything just sort of stopped for an embarrassing minute or two, when nobody dared to say anything.

Jade broke the tension by stating the obvious. "Marissa, how far along did you say you are? Eight months? I was looking at your belly, and you've dropped! It won't be long now."

Marissa rubbed her belly and said, "I've got a month, and my sister and mother went a whole two weeks past their due dates with their children. Don't worry; I'm not going to break the water on your sofa or anything."

Good, thought Max, then there will be no actual water involved with this baby shower.

"I'll go get the guest rooms ready," Max said, staring at Marissa's protruding bump. Max, who is used to being around giggling girls because of the cheerleaders, said, "I will take my breakfast upstairs, you enjoy this beautiful room and your baby shower planning," and he went to brood over what had changed in the dynamic with Isabella.

After breakfast, Max walked past his sister's room, where her friends were looking at different MOB dresses, giving their opinions.

"I was thinking, a summer wedding, we'd go for something like Town & Country meets Cosmo, a little class, a little glamour, lots of bling...but, no, she wants," and all the other cheerleaders repeated in unison, "simple, classic, and expensive!"

Max stopped and said, "Ah, is this the refrain about the plain and simple?"

"Yes, so plain, not even a little fluff piece thrown in to please her mama. She wants a plain white cake, costing what, the gross national product of some third-world country? And black and white photos, no color, and a band without any vocals, she wants a quartet, or was it an octet or a sextet...Just all plain, all simple, classic, and all very," she said, before the girls chimed in with her, "expensive."

Max had enough of the MOB sobfest and enough of Isabella's unexpected coldness this morning. He was going to take a shower and figure out how to get the fun back in this shore house. It was going to take more than a gaggle of gals and bad weather moving in to ruin his hiatus.

That evening, Max invited anyone left at the beach house to join him at the Yacht Club for a sunset dinner. Most of them would be leaving the next day, with only Max, Isabella, and Cyrus staying until Tuesday to prepare the house for the hurricane that was expected to pound the Jersey Shore on Wednesday.

Max wore a button-down Oxford shirt, khaki pants, and loafers; a kind of uniform for those sorts of clubs. He put on his suit jacket when he got to the entrance to the dining room, and instructed the hostess to ready his table for some of his favorite people.

Isabella, who was running late, came walking into the club. At the sight of her, a big smile crept across Max's face. The summer dress she wore was feminine and provocative, and a bit on the dangerous side if their relationship was strictly business, strictly platonic.

As the sun set over the bayside view, there was a lull in the conversation.

"Isabella, what about you?" inquired Ruth's mother, an artist and one of the most curious of the group. "Did I hear that you were engaged before? What happened, if I may ask?"

"Yes, do tell," giggled Julia.

Isabella felt like these cheerleaders were "level jumping" on their friendship. They were asking a deeply personal question, and they had just met. She pondered answering this personal question about a past failed relationship.

"I'm not really going to share all of the details, since that is sort of private," Isabella said, pausing to see if the ladies would get the hint that they were being intrusive.

Marissa, who wanted to save her friend from having to share the details, tried to be diplomatic, "Let's just say they had a difference of opinion about what Isabella meant when she said she was waiting for a ring on her finger."

Jade cut into the conversation, "I was away at college at the time, but I heard the scoop. Girlfriend here is very, uh, old-fashioned about the proper time to do things, if you get my drift."

"Didn't he just about take an engagement ring off of his grandmother's finger and plop it on yours and expect to get a present?" Marissa said in a quiet tone while looking at Max, realizing that there are males present.

She realized that Isabella was not getting into the spirit of the conversation and looked a bit abashed.

"Oh, I'm so sorry, Isabella, I thought that you just couldn't find the words…" Marissa apologized to her friend.

"Yeah," said Isabella, "it is hard to talk about." She took a deep breath, and decided to just get everything out there so that the conversation could move forward to another topic, hopefully something less intrusive and personal.

"We had a disagreement about the ring. I am traditional, and I told him I was waiting for a ring on my finger. I meant a wedding ring, though. I wasn't talking about an engagement ring, especially one that he filched off of his grandmother."

The girls all groaned and said things like, "What a loser," and "You're better off without him." Even Cyrus was mumbling reassuring comments like this.

Max, however, found himself groaning for another reason.

Chapter 14 - More of the Unexpected

"This house is not for rent."
Max Ivy to the renters at the door.

Shoring up the means to get a new identity and lifestyle, Rochelle was very grateful to secure Julia Ivy Mallory as a client. First of all, Julia was completely clueless when it came to the normal protocol of hiring and maintaining a working relationship with a wedding planner. Rochelle was able to finance today's trip to the Caymans and upcoming offshore surgical procedures with the unwritten deposit checks.

The great thing about this line of funding is that it didn't need to stop with the trip overseas. With the Internet, and some well-placed searches, Rochelle, formerly known as Regina, was able to get a listing number and interior photographs of the beach house that these spoiled rich and pampered people owned. They probably only visit two weeks of the year, anyway.

The next morning, the doorbell rang repeatedly. This time, Cyrus was able to answer the door.

"Hello, we aren't expecting guests. Who may I ask is calling?" Cyrus inquired.

At the doorstep was a very perplexed couple. "Hi," Dr. Cornea put out his hand, "I'm Dave and this is my wife, Sheryl. We have the place for the week. The whole house I was told."

As Max walked to where the visitors were arriving, he realized that there was a mistake.

"I'm sorry, you must have written down the wrong address. This house is not rented out, but many on the island are," Max explained.

Dr. Cornea put down his bags, and took out a computer printout. Pointing to the address and the map, and showing the receipt for the rental fee, he said, "Stop pulling my chain. Is this some kind of April fools-in-July joke? Aren't you that guy from TV? Are we being scammed?"

Max took a look at the papers, and said, "You aren't an eye doctor, are you?"

"No," the quiet Mrs. Cornea replied, "He's a veterinarian. I, however, am an attorney. I'm prepared to file a lawsuit if you don't let us in. We had a long car trip from New York and I have to pee. Please find someplace to put these bags unless you want us to call the police."

Max, for the second time in as many days was asked to carry bags, and wondered where Cyrus sulked off to this time. He realized that his henchman had been behaving rather oddly the last few days. With Isabella in a dither, too, and the shore house being up to the roof in professionals, it didn't seem like anything could get worse. And then, it did.

After Max brought the bags up to the fourth wing of the house, Max was grateful that the home was so palatial.

Cyrus returned, with his laptop computer in hand. "I've been checking out this rental scam, and the vet is right, he did put down a deposit. The scam was originated in the Caymans by someone posing as Julia. I have some friends with Interpol who are pursuing the lead as a favor for me. But, man, it looks like your sister is being scammed by a professional. Can you ask her if she knows anyone named Richie Scorcher?"

"Oh, and boss, the weather channel is saying that the storm is heading our way earlier than expected," Cyrus reported. "We may want to board up the place early, with there being so many glass surfaces."

Max went to find Julia in the breakfast room, asking Ruth for her mushroom and sun dried tomato quiche recipe.

While the name Richie did not ring any bells, Julia identified the last name as belonging to the wedding planner hired to make Charlene the most talked about bride of the Main Line.

As the wind started picking up, the Cornea family retired to their room for the night. They had been contacted by Interpol and apprised of the scam situation, and realized that they were unwitting victims. While they had hoped to have a whole estate to themselves, they recognized that at that price, it was probably too good to be true. They reconciled themselves to the hospitality of a rich Hollywood star with friends, which included a caterer. With gourmet meals by Ruth, and a future rife with possible litigation with this Richie person, they enjoyed the bay view, despite the storm clouds rolling in.

Marissa, however, started to feel mild contractions. Ruth and Julia offered to help time them, and to keep her well-hydrated. The contractions started to come more rapidly, firing at one every six minutes.

Her doctor's instructions had been to call the hospital when the contractions were less than five minutes apart, but, she was traveling. She decided to ask Isabella to call the closest hospital to ask the doctors what she should do.

While Isabella was on the phone trying to dial the hospital, Marissa let out a loud, blood-curdling scream! "She's coming; I can feel her head pressing down on me!"

Isabella was trying to decide whether to call for an ambulance, or just bring Marissa over to the hospital herself. Then she remembered that Max's vehicle didn't have any doors.

At that point, Max decided to rouse Dr. Cornea from his sleep.

As the sound of the loud wind mingled with the nearing sounds of the ambulance, a scrubbed up Dr. Cornea came down the steps while his wife came down with a pile of towels.

Cyrus, at the urging of Marissa, used his computer to track down a surprised Sid. While across the Atlantic, he quickly connected through Skype to communicate with his heavily laboring wife.

"Just a few pushes," said an experienced Dr. Cornea. "I've delivered many, many kids, but this will be the first human one," he quipped.

As the cries of a newborn baby came forth, Dr. Dave's wife rushed forward with the towels and cleaned off the infant.

"Let's call her Ivy," said Sid from "across the pond". Ivy raised her little fists in protest and wailed loudly.

Max watched how enthralled Isabella was with the whole upbeat and happy mood of the surprise early arrival of a gloriously perfect and adorable specimen.

As the baby gently snuggled against her mother's breasts and took her first drinks, a quiet calm descended over the room.

The EMTs finally arrived to take Marissa and the baby to Atlantic Hospital. Jade grabbed Marissa's hospital bag from the trunk of her car.

Then the wind and rain started to pick up considerably outside. Suddenly, one of the EMTs came in from outside, drenched from head to toe.

"We have been advised that everyone needs to shelter in place until after the storm has subsided," he said.

Chapter 15 - Ivy in the Storm

"Why do something yourself when it can be delegated?"
Julia Ivy Mallory to her daughter, Charlene

While the hurricane had been downgraded to a tropical storm, there was still a need to stay indoors through the rest of the night until the weather advisory was lifted.

Isabella was unable to sleep. All the emotions from observing a real live birth, plus her pool game with Max, had her keyed up.

She was wearing one of the cute nighties that Marissa had passed along to her, covered by her pink flannel robe. It was chilly, and she tied the comfortable fabric tight at her waist.

As she entered the kitchen hoping for a midnight snack, she noticed she wasn't alone. Max was there eating grapes and slices of cheese with crackers. He was wearing dark green monogrammed pajamas and fleece slippers.

"Isabella, care for a snack?" Max asked.

"Sure," she replied. "By the way, I need to apologize for my recent behavior."

"It's okay, I'm sure I did something to deserve it." Max replied, "I can be a knucklehead sometimes. May I ask what got you so annoyed?"

"It was what Charlene said on the phone....it is just that I feel so, I guess the word is "belittled," by your dad. I am just fed up with being second fiddle to you rich estate people. I have a lot to offer this world, a whole lot of God-given talents," Isabella tried to explain.

"Yeah, my dad is a total snob. But, Isabella," Max urged, "I'm not like that, and neither is Charlene."

"Well, it is also that Charlene said that we are dating, and I don't date anymore," Isabella explained, with sadness in her voice.

"Well, Isabella, whatever you want to call it, I do like you," Max put a comforting hand around her shoulder and brought her in for a hug. "And, I'd like to get to know you better. And, yes, I would like to date you."

"Well, I'm also kind of confused. There are things you need to know about me if we are," Isabella's voice was shaky, "if we are dating. I'm a virgin. I plan on waiting until I'm married," Isabella revealed. She was expecting to get the jilt, as so often happened when she shared this news.

Isabella had been on hundreds of first dates. She was beautiful, friendly, and most guys drooled at the thought of going out with her. But, when they found out that she wore, what was in essence, a non-material chastity belt, they quickly moved on. There was one guy who didn't believe her, and thought she was just a tease. After having kicked him where it hurt, she decided that all men were after one thing and that she would become a nun.

"I guess this is where you say that it was nice knowing you," said Isabella.

"Huh? I was just thinking about how unusual it is that you have saved yourself for marriage. That is so uncommon. But, you are a treasure, rare and beautiful. I kind of like the idea that you are treating yourself that way."

Max looked deeply into Isabella's eyes. "But, I am not going to lie and say that this isn't going to be a challenge for me."

"See, that is what I mean. All men are looking for just one thing. You think what I am saying is a challenge. You are going to try to seduce me…and, from the looks of it, seduce me with food. But I have to say that I am not seducible. Others have tried and failed," Isabella explained with a coy smile on her face.

"Isabella, I'm not other men." Max looked at her, taking her hand, and kissing it gently. "I have been around all kinds of depravity. Women are throwing themselves at me because I'm the newest celebrity. They send me their perfumed panties - it is disgusting. If waiting is what I have to do to be with a normal, sane, nice girl, then wait is what I will do. Let's just take things one day at a time."

Max, knowing that patience was a virtue of which he had very little, knew that this would be difficult. But life without Isabella looked bleak and abysmal. He would take his chances with frustration, cold showers, and whatever else was in store. For now, he would enjoy a refreshing snack with a beautiful girl, as the wind howled outside.

Chapter 16 - The Abduction

"You're getting too Type-A, you need to settle your soul."
Isabella upon "man-napping" Max

Max could not forget about the intimate kisses in the billiards room at Long Beach Island. He craved more time to get to know Isabella. He knew, however, that she was still seething from the unkind note from his father.

Oh, how Max wanted to give his father a piece of his mind!

However, he knew this needed to be done face-to-face. It had been almost ten days since he had seen Harrison Alexander Ivy, who was consumed by an overseas project and leaving very early in the morning for his office in Center City. Harrison was eating dinner at the Republic Club, the stalwart politically oriented stuffy old patrician gathering place in the city.

It was five in the morning, and Max was still thinking of Isabella. He was supposed to be getting ready to go for a "guy's day" with Jimmy, to get to know his soon-to-be nephew-in-law. Sporting a baseball cap, t-shirt, jeans, and waterproof mud-boots, Max was told to dress for a day of fishing on the Delaware River. This explained the early morning departure time. They were also going rock climbing at a gym, and to a Triple-A baseball game.

Max was pleasantly surprised to see Isabella drive up in a pickup truck. He thought about teasing her about girls driving trucks, but, realized that he was better off keeping his mouth shut. That was the sort of joke that made him feel superior to others, but in reality diminished him in other people's eyes.

"Did Jimmy send you to pick me up for fishing?" Max asked.

"No, I am abducting you." Isabella replied with a sly smile.

"Pardon me?" Max asked. "Am I dreaming?"

"You won't feel that way when you find out where we're going." Isabella replied.

Once they were both inside the truck, Isabella explained everything. The "guy's day" was a ruse; Jimmy was in on the abduction. This was because she won the bet and now they were "doing things her way."

"Now, get that smile off your face. It isn't that sort of abduction, and it isn't that kind of having my way." Isabella said.

The truck was needed as they traveled to the borough of Narberth for the annual Rummage Pilgrimage. On this one day each summer, residents left out all sorts of usable rubbish, from baby carriages to baby grand pianos.

Isabella asked Max to be on the lookout for anything usable in a garden or playground. They found several trellises for climbing plants, and a plaque that said, "There's no place like home."

When they were out of earshot from the "Narbs" – as he used to call them in his school years, Max asked, "And why are we picking through other people's garbage?"

"One, we need to stay on-budget for Charlene's garden, and there is no budget, so this is how we get something for nothing. Two, these nice items will look terrific in her garden and make it homey. Three, we are saving these items from ending up in the landfill."

"Oh, is this about that whole sustainability thing?" Max asked. "I guess these things are kind of cute, but it isn't like we can get any of our big-ticket items this way."

Thinking that their homage to shabby chic was over with mere "dumpster diving" at the sustainability pilgrimage, Max was dreaming about taking a cool dip in the pool at the Main Line estate.

Isabella, however, had other ideas.

As she drove the Albero Landscaping pickup truck west on Route 30, Isabella thought about how to best introduce the next destination to an unsuspecting Max.

"You need some buggy time," Isabella said to Max.

"Huh?" Max asked, "What's that?"

"You'll see," Isabella hinted, as she exited and got on the Route 30 bypass, heading towards Lancaster.

After a half-hour or so of driving, she skirted the highway and started taking some country roads through beautiful, rural scenery. The farms were large and old-fashioned, with laundry hanging from the lines in a variety of sizes and solid colors. The towns along Old Philadelphia Pike had corny, homespun names like "Bird-in-Hand" and "Intercourse."

Just as he was about to ask her if they were going to a farm, a carriage led by two brown mares appeared coming out of the driveway of the farm in the distance. In no time at all, the truck caught up with the buggy, which was moving along at a snail's pace.

"Let's see how long you can take it," Isabella said. "We'll call this a test of your patience. Whoever loses their patience first buys the other an ice cream."

Max, not one to lose a bet, imagined that the dairy farms in Lancaster County created the finest ice cream imaginable. He never complained, not once, about being stuck behind a buggy. They made it to the creamery in town, and Isabella, impressed, bought two scoops of his favorite flavor. She skipped on the ice cream, though. She wanted to look fit in the mint-colored bridesmaid's dress she would be wearing for Charlene's wedding. She was hoping that everything would go off without a hitch; there were just three weeks to go.

As Max and Isabella returned from Lancaster County, his cell phone rang. This time, he didn't put Charlene on speaker right away. "You're with Isabella," his niece said, "put me on speaker."

"Max, I want to ask you something. Since you are my favorite uncle in the world, will you walk me down the aisle?" Charlene asked.

Charlene explained that her father, Julia's first husband, Dr. Evan Mallory, would be unable to attend the wedding or walk his daughter down the aisle. He was expected to act as birthing coach for the birth of his second son from his third wife at her scheduled induced delivery.

Max was more than happy to do this. He knew that Isabella was doing a reading at the wedding, as well as serving as a bridesmaid.

As they drove past Lancaster County, Max saw more farmland and a sign that read "Berks County." Isabella backed the truck into an industrial-looking brick building with the name "Deluca Pavers" on the outside of the building. A six-foot ten, bald man came to meet her at the truck.

"Is Manny around?" she asked.

"No, he's freaking out today. Regina left for one of her plastic surgeries and didn't leave a note. He thinks she might have driven over a bridge or something. Poor guy, he's totally head over heels for her."

"All wives should be so lucky. Husbands should be devoted. I'm sure she'll be back really soon; she always is. Anyway, I heard that there is a pile of rejected fieldstone; I'm working on a garden and could use some."

"Sure, Isabella. We've got that in the back. You should have told me ahead of time, I would have had my driver load them up for you. As it is, he's working on the new supermarket complex. Did you hear about the project? We got the winning bid. I'd help out, but, you know, my back and all."

"Oh, that's OK. I brought some muscle here with me. Max, say 'Hello' to the nice paver man. Mike, just show us where the fieldstone is. Max and I will carry it out to the truck."

Once back on the road, Isabella called Jimmy on the cell to find out if the "coast was clear." He replied that Charlene was still visiting with her father and his new family, and she could drop the stones off. He had cleared space behind the compost pile for the stones, and they could drop them off and cover them with a tarp. If Charlene asked, he would make up a story about why the tarp was there. This garden would be kept a secret. Everything was going really well, except for Max, who realized that he would need to carry the stones to the back of the yard.

Max was bone tired by the time he arrived back at the Main Line estate. Wishing for a dip in the pool, or, at least a warm bath, he was agitated when Isabella said that he needed to make it quick. He would have to change his clothes, and then he would be making a public appearance at St. Agatha's.

"We're going to need to ask Cyrus to man up and make it to this shindig," Isabella explained. "He said he'd be ready to go at five, but I don't see him."

"Cyrus was in on this abduction?" Max asked incredulously.

"Sure. The rummage sale was his idea; they do something like that out in California where he's from…he thought it would give you a more global perspective."

"But, Isabella, I need to…" Just as he was about to give a whole bunch of reasons why he needed a backrub and not a church carnival, he saw a squad car drive up.

As detective McGovern got out of her squad car, she took a look at Max and said, "I am here representing the Lower Main Line Police. We have a warrant for the arrest of Julia Ivy on the charges of," she looks down at the warrant in her hands, "grand larceny."

As the detective rang the doorbell to the Ivy mansion, Cyrus walked up to Isabella and Max.

"Sorry I'm late," Cyrus said, "Julia has been getting lots of calls about bounced checks from her wedding deposits, and she asked me to look into things for her. It sounds like someone's taking her to the cleaners."

The checks to the reception site, caterer, and even tuition for Lacey's camp all bounced. Julia had given Lacey the camp experience as both a gift, and, as a way of acceptance that, yes, she was going to be a grandmother.

At that moment, Julia came out of the mansion in handcuffs. "Please call Uncle Spencer; he'll know what to do," she called out to Max.

"Isabella, I am sorry to beg off on the carnival, but I think my sister really needs me."

"But Max, I signed you up for the dunk tank, and they're charging $20 a dunk. We're really counting on you to get a new air conditioner for the gym, the children get really hot at summer camp, and the CYO kids…"

"Ah, Isabella, my sister was just led away in handcuffs, perhaps you could find another dunkee."

Isabella was adamant. "No way, who else is going to command a $20 a dunk fee? The nonnas are probably lined up around the block."

"Max, we need to go now to St. Agatha's, those kids are depending on you. I'll take the Hummer; we'll be there in no time at all. You can call your uncle along the way," said Cyrus.

"Isabella, perhaps you could go to the police station to see if there is anything else we can do for Julia."

"Cyrus, do you work for me or for her?" asked Max, feeling rather double-crossed.

"Well, boss, a bet is a bet." Cyrus answered.

Chapter 17 - The Incarceration

"I'm having a bad hair day, so can we hurry this up?"
Julia when having her rights read to her at the Ivy compound.

Julia was sure that this was just an accounting error, so she was not in the least bit upset. In addition, she knew that the Ivy name carried a lot of weight in the township.

Isabella went back to her place to take a quick shower and change into more suitable attire. She arrived at the police station, hoping that there was something she could do to help Julia.

As she waited in the seating area for a chance to ask if she could visit, she saw a distinguished gentleman who looked like he was a high-powered attorney.

"Oh, hi Flynn," Isabella said. "I haven't seen you since your oldest daughter's Baptism. How is she doing? I was wondering if I could visit with Julia Ivy, she was just arrested. I'm a friend of the family."

"Well, officially, no. But, unofficially, I am supposed to do anything that she asks barring giving her a nail file and the key to the cell. Some Phillies box tickets are riding on it, and they may even be in the post-season if we have a good year. Her attorney is here waiting. Julia said that she needs an hour of meditation to 'clear her karma,' but you are welcome to come back after that."

"Hello, I'm Julia's attorney," the gentleman said as he extended his hand. "Would you care to join me for a cup of coffee across the street?"

They walked to the diner and he ordered coffee. She asked for a cup of orange juice.

"I knew your mother; I was a fan of hers, and you look just like her."

"My mother was a seamstress; you must have her mistaken with someone else, unless you are a fan of finely tailored clothing."

"Yes, that's it. Miss, what did you say your first name is?"

"I'm Isabella Albero, and what is your name?"

"I'm Spencer Ivy, brother to Harrison. I'm Julia's uncle. Do you have any idea how she could have gotten herself in this predicament?

"Well, I have heard that Julia likes to delegate. Max once said she would have their nanny spread her toothpaste on the toothbrush, you know what I mean. Maybe someone who works for her messed up on their accounting."

"Grand larceny involves very large sums of money; it isn't just a check or two bouncing. The Ivy name holds a lot of clout around here, and, we can probably keep this out of the papers and off her record if we can figure out who did it. The name Albero sounds familiar, though. Oh, yes, that's the last name of the young man who is marrying Charlene. I couldn't make it to the engagement party because I was out of the country. You sure are the spitting image of your mother; does anybody else ever tell you that?"

"Sometimes people say that. I think it is a compliment…she was so beautiful. I miss her a lot. It is nice of you to remember your brother's gardener's wife."

Spencer took a deep breath and seemed distracted. "Indeed. Well, we must get back to this case. My son will be meeting us shortly to help with the investigation. Once we get to talk with Julia, it is critical that we discover the identity of the person who floated these wedding checks."

"Oh, I am sorry, I didn't realize this was connected to Charlene's wedding," said Isabella. "Of course, there was a wedding planner; I think her name was Rochelle. I never met her, but I hear she is a bleach-blond with big silicone lips and a Barbie-doll look."

"Sounds like the possible culprit. Oh, here's my son, now. Isabella Albero, meet Maximilian Bell Ivy."

An equally distinguished man, about 30 years old, shook her hand.

"I know, I know, you are wondering about the name. Maximilian was a popular name and my father and his brother both picked the name for their sons. Of course, at the time, neither realized that one was going to be a celebrity, and the other just a mere county barrister."

"Excuse me, son, but enough chit chat. We all get that you share a name with the other Max. Now, this issue is that Julia is in jail. We suspect her wedding planner, hired to plan for Charlene's wedding, of siphoning funds and floating bad checks."

"Father, excuse me, but grand larceny indicates a very large sum of money. Surely Julia would not have trusted just anyone with her check book."

When they were finally able to see Julia at the station, it was clear that she had done just that.

As the scope of Rochelle's scheme came to light, Julia realized that she needed to rethink her dedication to delegation.

As all of this commotion was going on at the police station, Charlene was in blissful ignorance. She returned from her trip to Northern New Jersey in a fit of excitement about her upcoming wedding.

She dreamed about the wedding that she had so carefully planned. She wasn't the type for ice-sculptures or princess tiaras. She was into simple elegance carved out of genuine love and commitment.

When she arrived home, she saw a drenched Max, looking like he had just been chased by a pack of wolves.

"Max, I've never seen you looking like a drowned rat. What's going on?"

"Isabella twisted his arm to get him to do the dunk tank at the church," Jimmy explained. But upon seeing the serious expression on Max's face, he quieted down. "What's going on?"

As Max explained where Julia was and why, he saw the crestfallen expression on his niece's face. She was going to have to put on a brave front for her husband.

"Is my mother okay? Has she called Uncle Spencer and the other Max?"

"There's another Max?" Cyrus inquired.

Chapter 18 - The Warning

"It took a lot of time to extricate myself from that mistake, and it took a big chunk of my fortune, too."
Spencer Ivy to his niece, Julia

Spencer asked to speak to his client in private.

"Julia, my dear niece, maybe this was all for the best."

"Well, granted, there are worse places to be, like, for example, a landfill…"

"No, I mean about the wedding. I think it might be providential that the wedding couldn't possibly happen now that the deposits have bounced." Spencer took a pause, and then calmly explained.

"Julia, you were too young to really understand what happened when I got together with Candace. She was just a silly auntie to you, and you never saw the bitter, vindictive side of her. Well, she dazzled us all at the beginning, me in particular."

Spencer then went on to describe his disastrous first marriage.

"The fact that a wonderful child came out of the carnage, well that was the saving grace of the whole decade. It took a lot of time to extricate myself from that mistake, and it took a big chunk of my fortune, too," said Spencer.

"What I am saying is that you might want to chalk this whole Albero thing off as a starter marriage, as a quick prelude to a more suitable relationship for Charlene. However, it isn't always so easy."

"Well, James is a very nice young man," said Julia. "He isn't at all like Candace. She was after your money, and willing to do anything to get it. Mother told me that Candace tricked you into getting her pregnant, and that is what a vixen does. She has told Max that story a million times, so that he doesn't "fall prey" to that kind of scheme. I know the whole story, but what does that have to do with Jimmy. He's a bit of a nebbish, I'll grant you that, but hardly a gold digger. Plus, he's gainfully employed, and in this economy, that's something. Aren't we supposed to be talking about my case? I'm here rotting away in jail while you reminisce about times long gone."

"But, dear niece, if someone had just stopped me before things got serious with Candace. There are ways that we can keep the ones we love from making mistakes. If only my brother had told me the doubts that he had about her…"

"Well, Uncle Spencer, if I ever make my way out of the cold dark cell that I'm currently calling "home," I promise to give that some good, long thought. Now, back to my case…"

"Well, of course. But, first, I must give you a word of wisdom about the Albero crew. Don't trust them. They are a dysfunctional bunch, there's all kinds of drug abuse and scandal in their past. He's got an aunt who…"

"Oh, really?" she admonished. "Almost every family around has a relative who has faced addiction, and it is a disease like any other. Please - this is every family in America, for goodness sakes! Look at the Betty Ford Clinic; it was named after a former first lady. When and if you dig up something truly juicy on James, let me know. Until then, can we please discuss my incarceration, or I will hire another attorney!"

"You can't afford another attorney, dear niece. So you need to consider my words wisely. I cannot and will not allow another disastrous arrangement in this family," warned Spencer.

"Isn't it Charlene you should be discussing this with? I'm not her keeper."

"I intend to do just that, after we get you safely out of jail," he said.

Chapter 19 - A Decision

"Maybe it is my turn to abduct someone?"
Jimmy expressing his desire to abscond with his fiancé

"Maybe this means it's my turn to abduct someone?" Jimmy said.

"Pardon me?" Max inquired.

"Not you. I love you like a brother, don't get me wrong, but you've been kidnapped enough today. No, it is your delightful niece, Charlene. I want to marry her right away. Char, how about it, want to take a car trip to Elkton, Maryland tonight?"

"If they aren't open 24 / 7, there's always a plane trip to Vegas," Cyrus offered, ever in a West Coast mentality.

"I'm not going to let this Rochelle woman mess up my wedding plans. Maybe the sites will honor our commitments," said Charlene.

"No can do. They won't stay in business if they allow that. But, if we're lucky, we'll get them to drop the charges, so Julia can be done with this mess. It's Francois that is the most strident in his charges, he feels taken advantage of," replied Jimmy.

Charlene was nervous. "Oh, how I had to beg Francois to do this for me! He kept telling me it is so unusual, and out of the ordinary. "Francois doesn't cater,' he kept saying. I was just so persistent. Oh, Francois…What will I do?"

"I'm sure your parents would be happy to allow you to have a wedding ceremony at your house, and Ruth Abrams would probably cater for you if you ask," Isabella said, reassuringly.

"Oh, then it will always be the Ivy wedding instead of the Albero wedding, that's exactly what I didn't want." Charlene said.

"Oh, what a happy problem!" said Cyrus. "You two love each other, you want to get married, and you'll find a way."

Just then, Julia walked in. "I'm free! Francois dropped the charges and so did the rest. Between you and me, I think father offered him box tickets if the Eagles make it to the Superbowl."

"Ah, the wheels of justice moving extra fast for the jet set, got to love the Main Line." Isabella said.

"Listen, I'm home, but we have a problem. Uncle Spencer is bent on breaking you two up, Jimmy and Charlene. He is coming to try to talk Charlene out of it. He says he has some sort of proof that the Albero family is a bunch of no-good con artists, or something like that. I just sort of tuned him out when he got all bent out of shape. But, we really should try to get this show on the road before he gets here."

"Show on the road, Mom. Whatever do you mean?" asked Charlene.

"Well, you *are* going to elope, aren't you? It will be so romantic, I just can't wait to tell my friends!"

"Why the rush, mother? You know I can hold my own against Uncle Spencer." Charlene replied.

"Once the news spreads that you have eloped, there won't be any gossip about the lost funds, missing deposit money, or anything like that. All the wedding details will be wiped clean with a simple phrase, 'They eloped!'" Julia explained.

"Well, that decides it, then." Jimmy responded. "We must do this for the sake of your mother, her reputation, and my sanity."

"Uncle Spencer will probably just follow along to Elkton, he's no fool. That's where he and Candace got married three decades ago, by the way," said Julia.

Cyrus and Max started to converse quietly, and then when they agreed upon the course of action, they explained their discussion.

"We are going to do a simple fake out. It happens all the time in Hollywood. Celebrity rides in one car to real destination, and look-alike decoy goes to another place to get the paparazzi off course." Max explains.

"And the decoy in this case will be?" Isabella asked.

Chapter 20 - On The Run

"They may even be connected to the mob."
Spencer trying to persuade "Charlene" not to marry Jimmy

Once they were sitting in the back seat of Jimmy's Nissan Altima, with Cyrus driving in the front, Isabella relaxed a bit.

"By the way, Max, how did it go with the nonnas?"

"Terrific, they loved me. I think the kids will get their air conditioning after all. By the way, you look great in Dior."

Isabella was wearing one of Charlene's trademark suits, for this occasion in white. Max had taken a very quick shower and put on one of Jimmy's work suits.

"You really think your Uncle Spencer will follow us to Elkton instead of going to the airport? I am so happy for Jimmy and Charlene, it is great that they can do the whole Parisian theme there in Vegas."

"Not to worry, even if he did catch up with them, they would be able to stand their ground. They're in love," sighed Max.

Once Max and Isabella arrived at the wedding chapel, they were told that it was closed and would open again early in the morning. Wanting to continue the charade and throw Uncle Spencer off the trail, they decided to stay in a hotel room overnight. With one room reserved for Max and Cyrus, put in Jimmy's name, and another room reserved in Charlene's name, to be used by Isabella, they were ready for any contingency.

Since Spencer Ivy would most definitely make initial contact with his grand-niece Charlene, Max felt it would be best to spend time in Isabella's room. He wanted to hold the fort for his favorite niece, and, Isabella was easy on the eyes. He enjoyed spending time with her and being in her presence, and looked for any reason to do so.

"Want a foot rub?" Max asked Isabella, who was taking off her shoe and giving her foot a little pinch as she stood by the window to the outdoors.

"Sure, but not right now. I think I see your uncle walking towards the main entrance. He has a scowl on his face. I'm glad you're here to watch my back." Isabella said.

"Honey, I'll watch your back anytime, speaking of …" Max was interrupted by a loud pounding at the door.

"Charlene, I know you're in there." Uncle Spencer intoned.

"Yes." Max, imitating Charlene's high-pitched voice, replied from behind the door. Isabella stifled a hearty laugh.

"I just can't let you marry that fellow. I know he seems perfectly nice, but there's lots of baggage that you are unaware of. Open the door, there are some truths you need to hear, dear." Spencer said.

"No way, you're just making things up. You just don't like that he's a regular guy and not a member of the jet set." This time it was Isabella who pretended to be Charlene.

"I don't want to broadcast your business all over this hotel hallway, but I guess I must. I can't let you marry that young man. Look at that family he comes from. His father had ties to organized crime and died in a mysterious way." Spencer said. "Why else do you think Jimmy and his mother go by her maiden name, Albero? That name is synonymous with landscaping around the Main Line, but his father's last name is synonymous with organized crime. She wouldn't be hosting a TV show with that last name; people know what they are about," he said.

At this affront to her late uncle Joel, Isabella opened the door and confronted Spencer. "First of all, Mr. Ivy, my uncle Joel was a well-respected member of the community. Secondly, he was killed by a hit and run driver. It was a tragedy. And third, this is a bunch of ethnic stereotyping and slander. Italian-Americans have contributed to this country in countless positive ways! We helped build the bridges you drive on, we are astronauts and Supreme Court judges, and…well, you get my point!"

"I see…so you and Max are trying to throw me off the track. Well, I just want to self-advocate. I am doing this because I care deeply about my family and I don't want to see them make the same mistakes that I did. Now, you owe me this much, Max. Who gave you the money for that rowing trip to England back in college? Quid pro quo, here. Tell me where Charlene and James are?" demanded Spencer, who felt entitled to a reply.

"Max doesn't owe you a thing," Isabella interjected.

"Yes, Uncle Spencer," Max said. "I think it is your turn to man up. You've gone too far this time; you owe Isabella an apology for these lies and innuendo. Plus, I think you should take us out to dinner. I'm hungry, and you owe it to us. He looked down at his watch. "And Jimmy and Charlene should be touching down in their destination right about now, and it is too late for you to stop them, so we have a wedding to celebrate!"

Chapter 21 - The Reception

"Truth be told, I enjoyed each and every moment of those escapades. I never felt so alive." Max to Isabella at the reception

Charlene and Jimmy made it to Vegas, got hitched, and then called home with the news and information about their return flight.

When the happy newlyweds returned to the Ivy mansion, everything was in disarray. There was a note saying that Harrison and Camille were putting together a reception at The Saxon Country Club for the immediate family, and that they should join them there.

The country club opened up the dance floor and a speaker system was set up to play music. As Isabella and Max danced and danced some more, they were totally in sync and moved gracefully together.

Max took a break and headed to get refreshments for himself and his parched dancing partner. His mother pulled him aside.

"Max, think about what you are doing. You are returning to California next week. It would be cruel to get into anything serious."

"Mother, you are, and have always been a snob," he said, and started to walk off.

His father stepped in and said, "Listen to your mother; she has something of importance to say."

Camille added, "Yes, son, I do. I am not, nor have I ever been overly status conscious. This isn't about all that social class mumbo jumbo. Isabella is, like so many of the people who live around here, provincial. She will live here her whole life. But you, you son are a citizen of the world."

"Gee, Mother, is the sort of world I come from the kind where people make up false stories about the dead and lie and steal to get their way? If so, maybe I need to be more like Isabella and less of the world," Max retorted.

He waited for that to sink in and then stormed off. He ended up walking a distance to the edge of the woods that surround the country club. Coincidentally, that is where he found Isabella.

"Hi," said Max, "I guess we have a similar response to social gatherings - find the nearest way out."

"Yes," Isabella said, breaking from her train of thought. "I have been putting a lot of things in God's hands and using the power of prayer. I…" She stammered a bit, unsure of the words. "I need to apologize to you. I was so cruel to you at the shore. You are not your father. It is unfair for me to judge you on the basis of his mistakes."

"Isabella, all my life my parents have tried to select activities, friends, even professions that they feel are worthy of me. Some part of me always felt that they did this because they cared about me. But, the truth is that they cared about their own reputation and status, and saw me as a vehicle to enhancement of these things. The labels of the clothing that I wore, the name of the colleges that I attended, this meant more to them than anything. The real me, the man inside, was never of importance, Isabella," Max explained, "When I'm with you, I feel so alive and so real."

Looking out at the expansive greenery at The Saxon Country Club, Max put a protective arm around Isabella's waist. An autumn breeze rustled through from the surrounding woods.

"Max, I am sorry that your parents are not more supportive of you the way you are. You are a very special person. Does this mean that I am forgiven for the way I ordered you around at Long Beach Island, and the tricky way I swindled you in billiards, and the time I abducted you?," she asked.

"Apology accepted. Truth be told, I enjoyed each moment of those escapades. I never felt so alive. Please, get to know me better. I think we have a lot in common." Max said. "For one thing, we both grew up in the same place."

Isabella was flooded by memories of childhood, of dreams of pony rides and fantasies of her youth, back when she lived at the Ivy estate and anything was possible.

Maxed turned to face her, and asked her if she had ever considered living anyplace other than the Main Line, as this area was where she had always called home.

"I have always wondered what it would be like to garden in a different climate zone, but I think I'd miss my dad and the company we have worked so hard to build," she answered honestly, touched by his keen interest in her inner workings. "Why do you ask?"

Just as Max, who was nervous and a bit dizzy by this point, was about to ask a very pressing, personal question, there was an announcement over the speakers of the sound system.
"The Bride and Groom are about to cut the cake! Come to the portico, everyone!"

Their moment of solitude lost, they headed to see Jimmy and Charlene cut their cake.

Although some folks still snicker about Jimmy and Charlene's low-scale honeymoon, others were touched and found it hopelessly romantic. The North Beach shore house, each room decorated to represent a different country, was the perfect destination for the very much in-love couple.

But, while Jimmy and Charlene relaxed and unwound, the rest of the family was actively involved in renovating and reinventing the garden space of the newlyweds' home.

Chapter 22 - Finally Getting Down and Dirty

"The reason that I love fountains is that they symbolize hope. Throw your pennies in the fountain and make a wish upon a fountain, and it will happen."
Julia describing her penchant for garden statuary

"Ah, I see you go gloveless, too." Max remarked, as he set to work beside Isabella planting the foundation shrubs along the mulched border.

"Can't find a pair of gloves that let me get the precision that I get without them," she explained.

"Isabella," Max stopped what he was doing to look her in the eyes, "it took me a while, but I *do remember* you from high school. I think I need to apologize, and explain for myself. You always seemed so overly serious, and I just wanted to see you smile. I sensed that there was a playful side to your personality, and it bothered me that you were never in the crowd just having fun."

"My mom passed away when I was in eighth grade. It was devastating. I think it took me a long time to get over her passing," she said.

"I didn't know. Oh, I'm so sorry. Well, that might explain why my dad wanted you and Dan off the estate." Max said.

"Why is that? He wanted to make us suffer even more? He felt we needed more trials and tribulations?"

"No. I know my father, and he is very possessive. He may not have wanted a single, handsome man like your dad around his wife. Maybe he thought my mom had a tender heart towards your dad, or something."

"Your father is possessive all right. He thought my dad stole $500 bucks! Either way, it is over and done with."

"I can't excuse the bad things that my dad did and said," Max explained, "but I can ask your forgiveness. Also, I can ask you to consider giving me another chance. But, if it isn't me that you are looking for, please don't give up on having a good relationship. There has to be someone out there who is just right for you."

"Well, that ship has sailed, too. All I hear is 'You're a nice girl, but,' and then it is excuse, excuse, breakup. I'm sick and tired of being the nice girl doormat," she said.

"Don't give up on dating; there are nice guys out there who will respect your waiting," Max assured her.

"Sure, they'll respect it. Then, they'll conveniently lose my phone number," replied Isabella, sullenly.

"Well, I think what is missing in our society is restraint." Max replied. "I've got randy fans throwing panties at me. It gets me thinking, there has to be something more to life than this. Relations between men and women should be a spiritual undertaking."

"You mean Max Ivy has a spiritual side?" Isabella asked.

"Isabella, take a good look at this chrysanthemum flower we're planting. No, don't deadhead the few wilted ones, just really focus on the vibrant petals, bursting with vitality. The Chinese call that "chi," which loosely translates to 'life force.' All living things have it." Max explained. "Sure, I have a spiritual side."

"I got acupuncture to help with some repetitive joint pain and the holistic practitioner, Roxanne Laurento, also does some shiatsu massage. She talks about chi all the time. There are meridians through the body and sometimes she even gives my feet a massage. I love that, she said."

"Well, I would offer to give you foot rubs any old time you ask. But, first, let me show you some stretches for gardening that my personal trainer taught me. They prevent some of those repetitive injuries, especially back strain," Max said.

Max demonstrated some stretches which highlighted his limber and lithe limbs. As he moved his elbow above his head to demonstrate a tricep exercise, she felt a jolt of heat. She was starting to forget about the reason for these moves, getting in shape for gardening, and got distracted by Max's form.

However, Isabella was taken out of the moment by the sound of her aunt's voice. Anya, who never enjoyed gardening in the least, was offering some help in this project.

Anya Albero, Jimmy's busy mom, came over to say "Hello" and to offer her kind of help. "These flowers were left over from our home and garden show, and were too shabby to sell after all the manhandling they got on the set."

"Ah, you mean they are "Spokesmodel-Hydrangeas?" deadpanned Max.

"Well, I consider it more like a "Save the Seals" type of thing, I mean, it is pretty droopy," answered Anya.

"I'll perk them up with a special plant tonic Dad taught me years ago," said Isabella.

"Where is that brother of mine, I thought he'd be in his glory here, and he's always been close to his nephew, my Jimmy," Anya said.

"He's helping an apple orchard near Morgantown to go organic. Get a kick out of this, the owner's name is Candy, and Dad calls the farm "Candy Land," said Isabella.

Anya chuckled and bid them farewell.

"Hmm," commented Max, after a period of silence.

"What's "Hmm" supposed to mean?" asked Isabella.

"Well, is she single?"

"Yeah, are you interested?" Isabella replied.

"No, but your dad might be. You said just the other day that he seemed so distracted lately. Maybe he's smitten. Besides, Candy's not my type."

"Oh, really? Then what, exactly, is your type?" she asked.

"Someone passionate, lovely, and currently covered from head to toe in mulch." Max teased.

He cupped his dirt-covered hands on her face, kissed her succulent mouth, and took her breath away.

"Really, Isabella, you must reconsider this not-dating thing. You're just too young to give up on the dream of happy forever after. There's plenty of time for us to get to know each other and see."

"Max, age has nothing to do with it. When it comes to dating guys, I've been burned."

"Well, I'd like to show you how to deal with that very problem," he teased, as he started a playful water fight.

"You two kids, what kind of work ethic is this? I leave you in charge, Isabella, and you look like you've taken up mud wrestling." It was Dan, teasing his all-grown-up Pumpkin.

He stopped by, with his "arm Candy."

"Is my sister around?" Dan asked, "I want to introduce her to Candy."

"She had to leave so that she could fill in for the jewelry show host who had complications following a, uh, particularly unnecessary plastic surgery," said Isabella.

"Oh," replied Candy, "I heard about that on the entertainment news. She was augmenting her, um…I can't say it in mixed company."

"Well," said Gardener Dan, "as long as she isn't hawking plants, I'll keep watching. I love my sister, but she knows nothing about flowers.

The whole time we were growing up she refused to do anything that would get dirt under her fingernails."

"Yeah," replied Isabella, "I even gave Aunt Anya a really nice pair of garden gloves from Olivia's Gardens one year for her birthday. She gave them back with a note that said they would scratch up her polish and that I would put them to better use. I still have them, but, as you can see, I prefer to garden without them."

"Heavens, you're covered in grime, but pretty as the day you were born," replied her doting father.

"Good thing it is an "Indian-Summer" day, because you'll need more than a water fight to clean up. You're going to need the hose. In fact, I think we'll leave you two to that. I'll take Candy over to the studio to catch Anya at her next break."

Upon their return to Wayne, Charlene and James were reunited with Lacey, who had a great time with Grandmother Julia and didn't miss camp one bit. The three of them were treated to a big reveal. The exterior of the suburban home was completely upgraded and emanated charm and grace.

The garden was sustainable, using local native plants and recycled decorative elements. Lacey was given a new play set, built into a tree, as a gift from her now great-grandmother, Camille. And, at the insistence of Julia, who threatened to give away the surprise if she didn't get her way on this, there was some garden bling. A hand-carved tree stump in the shape of a rooster, several crystal wind chimes, and two stone fountains rounded out the décor.

The landscape was not a complete surprise to Charlene, but she was very pleased. However, she found the fountains and the stump carving to be ostentatious, and thus not entirely to her liking.

Chapter 23 - The New Normal

"It's just another Manic Monday"
-Written by Prince, Sung by The Bangles

Isabella was daydreaming about Max and his exciting way with the trowel…

She had enjoyed getting to know Max, and was sad that he was returning to Los Angeles in a few days. He had been able to break through her tough exterior, and learn about the soft woman inside.

She thought with longing about Max, recalling the ways he kept limber to prepare the body for all the digging and bending involved. He had showed her some gardening stretches, and even demonstrated them for her at Jimmy's site. She thought about Max's tremendous physique, and how much power he amassed when he did physical tasks like edging and…She was letting her mind get away from her. He would be returning to his gilded television lifestyle shortly, and, for all she knew, a bevy of Los Angeles chippies.

But she thought it was time to return to reality and forget all about this romantic silliness. As she sorted through the "snail mail" addressed to the office, she saw several thank you notes from Charlene and Jimmy for the beautiful garden. Last week's big reveal had been one of the highlights of Isabella's life. Isabella placed the notes from her cousin and his new bride into a scrapbook, wishing that she would have more opportunities to bring her talents to her family.

Then, she switched to sorting through the faxes and emails, and forwarded the landscaping and tree service correspondences to Dan. She had not seen much of him lately; he seemed rather distracted and occupied, but he was doing his job professionally and amiably as always.

Isabella took care of the mail that was related to design requests and questions. She noticed an unusual query for a design project in New York City. While she had frequently received these requests, she usually referred these clients to another landscape designer she knew who made frequent trips for jobs in the Big Apple, Patrick Lanzetti. This particular job, however, was rather enticing. It was a sustainable rooftop vegetable garden, and it looked intriguing. Isabella set it aside for further consideration.

Then she resumed daydreaming about Max...

The man in question, Max, was sitting by the pool of the Ivy estate. He was using his wireless connection to contact his producers in Los Angeles, annoyed that it would take so long to hear back because of the darned time difference.

Finally ready to make significant changes in his part of the home improvement show, Max was hoping to use more environmentally friendly practices and sustainable materials. He thought about the cute way Isabella's nose had crinkled when she had told him, with distaste, about the peat moss bogs, which took thousands of years to regenerate. Who knew?

And who would ever have known that the down-home spunky brunette would be on his mind 24-7? She was getting to be like a habit, and it would be tough to leave her to go back to the whacky entertainment biz.

In years past, returning to Los Angeles was a big relief. His parents and their snotty world was something of which he generally wanted no part. But, now he was stuck on a sweet hometown lady. Who would have thought that this could happen to him?

Julia, back at the main house, was not sleeping restfully.

She was delighted to have married off her only child to a very nice man, and to have a lovely step-granddaughter upon whom to dote. The whole wedding and garden reveal had been delightful, despite serious obstacles and setbacks.

She was tossing and turning, however, because of a responsibility that she keenly felt towards someone awaiting the wheels of justice. Julia was upset at the notion that it was she who was deciding the fate of Charlene's wedding planner, Rochelle. Julia's lawyer and good friend, Henry Marks, had encouraged Julia to press charges against the schemer, who had stolen $15,000 from unpaid wedding deposits.

Rochelle had pocketed the money, and quickly fled overseas to begin her lifelong dream of becoming a Lady Doll, her favorite and only toy while growing up in the projects and then in foster care. Through a rigorous set of physical enhancements, she would have the tighter, firmer, newer, better self and she could easily be a trophy wife for someone like Spencer Ivy, or, maybe even a political candidate. Who knows? All it took was the right body. Her body, right now, was currently in a prison infirmary, as she healed from her latest procedure and awaited extradition from the Caymans.

Julia fell back restfully to sleep, having made the decision to drop the charges. A crowded prison was not the right place for someone in the midst of healing. And, who was she to stand between someone and their dreams?

Cyrus woke up early, which was his preference, and checked his messages. He had friends in all levels of law enforcement, and was eager to check his machine to see if his contacts had resolved any of the discrepancies in this new investigation. Her off-beat intensity about the environment had him thinking that Isabella Albero was knee deep in banana peels.

Who would have thought that his research into the sending of banana peels signed by "PETE" would have resulted in the prime suspect being his boss's new love interest?

An enigma, this Isabella woman was.

On the surface, she appeared quite like a paragon, a status-quo God-loving, God-fearing Catholic, Julie Andrews-climb-every-mountain type of girl. A church mouse, a quiet, non-rule breaker, she was someone who would be off the radar screen of any sort of investigation.

It was only when he looked beyond the veneer that some discrepancies began to appear in her bio.

He decided to mix business with pleasure and look into his suspect by meeting with her spicy best friend, Jade.

Jade had worked through the weekend, since movie making was an intense proposition. As assistant producer at a King of Prussia film studio, she was expected to be living and breathing cinema.

Her glamorous but intense job entailed making vital decisions about which scenes to keep, and which to leave on the cutting room floor. Even though everything is digital now, it still meant that someone, an actor or a writer, usually, would be displeased to find out that a particular moment or whole scene was eliminated from a production. And, those disappointed, pissed off people would feel like they were being left on the cutting room floor. Well, Jade wasn't making any friends at "Philly Cinema," but she was getting "The Forecast" to the quality of film noir that made Academy Award dreams a possibility. In the end, all would be forgiven!

The movie was sure to be an attention-getter. It was a terrifying look at what the world would be like in 30 years if alternative sources of energy weren't developed and widely implemented.

She pushed her chocolate-colored ringlets out of her hazel eyes, and wiped the perspiration from her brow. This was exciting work, and it made her projects at film school look like child's play.

All of a sudden, she felt a climate shift in the room. It was as if her neck was tingling and the hairs were standing on edge. She turned around and saw a devastatingly handsome man watching her closely.

"I hope you have good insurance," He said, his smile indicating that this was a barb.

"Oh," she drawled, "Why's that?"

"With scenes like that, people are going to be having heart attacks in the theater," said the mystery man.

As he got closer, Jade recognized Cyrus, the beefy bodyguard from the shore. But what was he doing in the studio?

"Hi Jade. You're just the person I came to see. I'm doing an investigation for Max," he said, with a toothy grin.

"I have a lunch break coming up, can you meet me in the break room?" she asked. "It is down the hall to the left. Help yourself to a soda can." Jade said.

"Never touch the stuff. And, from where I come from, it is called by another name. But thanks just the same," Cyrus explained.

A few minutes later, a freshened up Jade walked into the lounge bursting with curiosity and anticipation. She passed the hard-bodied, suited-up stud a bottle of water.

"Thanks, Jade. I'd like to ask that we keep this conversation confidential."

"Depends what is being said. I don't keep secrets from my home girl; we've been through too much for that. Besides, it is just too tough to keep things from someone's best friend. It is about Isabella, right?"

"I assure you that it is in her best interest to cooperate; I wouldn't want the police involved," Cyrus replied.

"What? You've got to be kidding. I thought you were going to ask me about the whole virgin thing. That's what is usually on a guy's mind when they ask me about Isabella. She's not anyone's criminal, I assure you."

"Well, I want to show you a letter that was received at Max's producer's office in LA. He hasn't seen it yet, and, hopefully, this matter can be settled quietly."

Jade took a look at the letter, which was written in handwriting that looked like chicken scratch. She read it aloud, "Prune this, you sucker! You've bleated the peat out of the environment, deadheaded the good wood, and <u>changed things that were just fine the way they</u> <u>were</u>, you moron! Deadhead this, PETE."

"It sounds like a fan on mushrooms; you can't be taking this note seriously," Jade responded.

Accompanying the bizarre note was a pair of pruning sheers, which, technically could be construed as a weapon.

"The pruning sheers were traced to a purchase made by Albero Enterprises, the company home of Albero Landscaping, and Isabella's company," said Cyrus.

Jade abruptly appeared to change the subject.

"Do you like animals?" Jade asked Cyrus.

"Uh, what do you mean, like as in eating? No, I'm a vegetarian," he said.

"No, I mean, have you ever given money to help keep animals from harm?"

"Sure," said Cyrus.

"We do a lot of work with that animal rights group, PETA, People for the Ethical Treatment of Animals, when on film shoots. Most film projects have animals involved, and I've actually worked closely with PETA to ensure that animals are not harmed in any way during a production," explained Jade.

"You've lost me on this," Cyrus said.

"Well, maybe 'Pete' is really an acronym of PETE, and it means People for the Ethical Treatment of something like, I don't know, the Environment, the Ecosystem, something like that," Jade explained.

"Interesting theory, Jade. It certainly bears looking into. And, you're an interesting girl. I think, as part of this investigation, we should discuss this further. What are you doing for dinner tomorrow night?"

"Well, I did have a date with the Eagles quarterback, but for you I'll change it to another day. Where did you have in mind?" she queried.

"You're a savvy local, you chose the place, just don't make it too casual, I'm *not* a t-shirt and jeans guy!" Cyrus was inwardly chuckling at the girl's audacity, knowing that the football player she mentioned, while handsome, was currently dating a supermodel.

"How's seafood sound, then?" She inquired. She selected a noteworthy seafood place in Manyunk, and they set a time to meet.

"Oh, Cyrus, two other things," Jade drawled, "First, Isabella has impeccable penmanship, and, secondly, there are *a lot* of people who think your boss is a moron."

Chapter 24 - Through the Main Elevator

"There's only one way into these buildings for us landscapers, through the service entrance."
Patrick Lanzetti to Isabella, explaining how things work in New York City

The next day, Isabella kept looking at the request for the rooftop garden project. This was a once in a lifetime opportunity, and she finally decided to take it. Besides that, she could use a diversion from the upcoming departure of her new love interest. She needed something to occupy her thoughts besides Max, who had also been starring in many dreams of late, too.

She wrote an email back to Mrs. Amy Crescent, who was creating a rooftop garden in the Chelsea section of Manhattan. She was looking to grow a sustainable, environmentally friendly vegetable garden. It sounded like a fun project.

Isabella had to see about the weight limits that the rooftop would allow, and it might mean a consult with a structural engineer. Crescent was willing to pay any expense that the project required, and she was also interested in using vertical elements, such as hanging plants and trellises.

Isabella decided to get started right away on the project, and she recalled that Patrick had worked on a similar rooftop. She decided to stop by the Lanzetti family compound to see if he was around.

As she turned the corner of New Devon Avenue, which was due east of her offices in Wayne, she noted that the geraniums were in bloom in front of the Lanzetti property. There must be thousands of these annuals lined up in front of the family compound and plant nursery. Pat's mom was proud of the homey touches that the flowers provided to the shared work and residential environment.

Patrick was outside, pruning a rose bush for his mom. Long-limbed and lanky, he walked with an unusual grace for a man who made his living in a blue-collar trade. Pat was well-read, well-groomed, and rather fussy about his clothing.

Isabella was wearing one of her new floral sundresses from Marissa, since she didn't have to do any digging today. There was no need to wear mud pants and boots. Her hair was freshly washed and combed, as opposed to its usual disarray. Her black dress was covered in flowers, and the strappy sandals she had bought at the shore matched perfectly.

Patrick looked up briefly from the rose and was astounded by what he saw. The demure church mouse that he had known for years was transformed into a vision of loveliness.

As she explained the reason for the visit, Patrick realized that something must have happened to instill this new confidence and daring in his colleague. However, he didn't really care what the reason for it was; he was just thrilled by her new look. "You know, Isabella, I have been going up to New York twice a week now, and I'd be happy to have some company on the ride up. We would need to stop at the tree farm in Doylestown on the way, but it would be a great way to catch up on things and get your project underway," Patrick said.

Isabella was familiar with the tree farm, as it featured the healthiest plants at the most affordable rates, and had a terrific web presence. She had not visited the farm in years, so this was going to be a real treat.

"The customer already mentioned that Tuesdays and Thursdays would be possible, so, I'm going to say yes." Isabella replied.

Isabella didn't know how people managed to drive in New York City, it was so congested and the drivers were so impatient. She said a silent prayer for a cyclist that was stopped at the intersection along with what seemed like hundreds of other motorists. She was grateful that Pat was at the wheel, even though she prided herself in her various drivers' licenses. There wasn't a type of vehicle that she didn't have the ability to drive, including monster trucks and motorcycles. However, she was intimidated by the sheer volume of movement, colors, lights, and sounds. It was overwhelming.

When they drove into the parking garage of the Ames high rise, Pat explained that it was customary for the building staff to bring the landscapers up the service entrance. He said that he rarely was in contact with the actual upscale urban dwellers that constituted his client base in the city.

As they approached the entrance to the parking garage, they saw an attendant dressed in a jeans and a white t-shirt emblazoned with "Ames Enterprises."

"Patrick Lanzetti," he said, extending his hand for a firm handshake. "We're here from Albero Landscaping, hired by Amy Crescent for the rooftop project."

Expecting to be shown to the service entrance, Patrick was surprised when they were lead to the main elevator and told to go to first floor.

"Willis Ennis," introduced the man, "superintendent of the building, and a budding actor," he said, as he unlocked the door to what lead to a series of open cubicles. He explained that this floor of the building contained the building management and hospitality offices, and that he had been managing the building for two years between auditions. He said that Mrs. Crescent would be with them shortly. He also asked about Patrick, saying that he didn't know that another landscaper would be coming.

"Fellow landscaper and friend," Patrick replied, "Isabella and I met at state college at the design school. I drove her up. My outfit does a lot of work up here, but we don't have her kind of creativity. You know the way the women have with sprucing things up really pretty.

Isabella appreciated that Pat did not divulge that she had just taken one course there, and that her degree was an Associate's Degree from Community College in Landscape Design.

The superintendent said to Isabella, "I am supposed to check your driver's license, to make sure that you are indeed Isabella Albero, born in April of 1978, and then I am to offer you this check as a first payment on the landscape design. Second payment for the same amount will be when you submit the plans to the structural engineer, and final payment of same said value when you revise the plans with engineering feedback."

"I've never been asked for my license before, but here it is," Isabella said. Ennis looked at the rough-edged woman in the photo and back to the polished lady in front of him, and said, "The camera does not do you justice!" He went over to make a Xerox copy of the license for his boss, circling the birth date, April 17, on the print out.

At this point, Isabella was handed a check for what was more than her average annual salary.

Taking a peek at the check, Patrick was amused. "This is one fun urban adventure," Patrick said, his eyes twinkling. His little church mouse was proving to be a spitfire. He realized, too late, that he was starting to fall deep for the sort of person that he had most explicitly swore himself off of - a marriage-minded female. It was too soon after his disastrous first marriage.

But she was so adorable in her sandals and sun dress; she looked so ripe for the picking.

Chapter 25 - Always Well–Suited

"I never dress casually, remember that."
Cyrus

At the beach, Jade had seen Cyrus in swim trunks, and she noticed that he was rock-solid muscle. She had taken a few glances his way, when she had the opportunity, which was rare. At LBI, he had been either catering to the whims of his boss, Max, or chatting it up with the twenty-something caterer, Ruth.

As Cyrus walked into the restaurant, several heads turned. He was dressed head to toe in black, and had the sleek look of a male model. His hair was slicked back, and he had a pale complexion and wolfish gray eyes.

As they sat at the table and perused the menu, Jade felt a need to get an idea of what her chances were with this stud du jour.

"You and Ruth looked a little cozy at LBI, what's the scoop?" Jade asked, expecting to get invited to their wedding in the Hamptons.

"Oh, Ruth, she's a nice girl, but too young for me. I am learning how to cook and she went to the Cordon Blue." Cyrus said, elusively. "Anyway, I have a few questions about Isabella, if you don't mind getting started right away."

"Oh, Isabella…Is that what this is about? Do you have a thing for her?" Jade asked, not one to skirt a confrontation.

"No. Most emphatically, no. She isn't my type."

"Well, she is really beautiful, I mean, once you get past the mud boots and grimy garden gloves. And, she's…" Jade defended.

"Totally not suitable for me, in any way," Cyrus explained.

"Well, I have a need to defend my girlfriend; if this is about the virgin thing…you men are all dogs." Jade said defensively.

"It is not her experience, or lack thereof, that is the issue for me. Although, I have to say, in this day and age, that is sort of refreshing, although hard to believe. But, anyway, it is her Catholicism that is the issue," explained Cyrus. "I practice Judaism, and will only date others who do, as well."

Jade thought about that, and said, quite unexpectedly, "Oh, what about someone who is half-Jewish?"

At that point, the waiter came to take their orders. Jade ordered a crab cake sandwich, and Cyrus ordered salmon with a side of broccoli.

"Anyway," Cyrus interjected, "The boss is quite smitten with your Isabella. It is a real pickle that she is the main suspect in some recent eco-harassment. All the clues keep pointing to her in terms of who is doing this environmentally whacko sending of stuff," Cyrus explained.

As Cyrus described the escalating bizarre cascade of banana peels, pruning implements, and other oddities, Jade decided to lay her cards on the table.

"Isabella is too demure, too prudish, and just plain too good to do anything so stalker-like. She might want to do it, she might dream about doing it, but would never go through with it. She's really timid. I think you might want to see who else works for Albero Enterprises. You know, I was familiar with the landscaping side, but I had no idea that there were other businesses," Jade commented.

She had been around the Albero family since she was ten and her parents split, and her mom moved back to Ardmore. Her dad, Arthur Baum, was now busy in Jersey with his second family and his second home, Temple Beth Hillel. She knew first-hand of the Albero landscaping dynasty, built from sweat, but had never heard of any sort of other business interests.

Cyrus described how Albero had diversified into limestone quarries during the booming times of the late 1990's, and had even recently gone into organic garden sprays and other products in the gardening trade. While all of the holdings were related directly or indirectly to gardening, they had come very close to the construction industry because of an overlap, and were involved in the manufacturing of pavers.

"So, you can look at the other people who work for these enterprises, then. That gives you something to do. Maybe there's some garden guru who hates the depletion of the peat moss bogs so much he is whittling tiny "Max'" in his spare time. There are lots of possible suspects! So, can we move this conversation to topics other than Isabella, or is there anything *else* you want to know?" an exasperated Jade said.

"Well, the investigation side of me is curious about this chastity thing. How can you be so sure she is a virgin? Isn't that sort of unheard of these days?" asked a curious Cyrus.

"You never knew her mother. If you did, you would understand."

The dinner was served, and Jade was annoyed at herself for having ordered something that wasn't kosher. How was she to know? And, of course, she had to suggest a seafood restaurant.

Daintily eating of the crab cake sandwich, she said, "It is not everyday you meet someone as wholesome as Isabella, that's for sure, but she is quite a tomboy. She's been able to hide behind the hydrangeas, and live the life that her mother planned for her. Let's see, where to start…Isabella's mother, Sharon Rose, was one of the most beautiful women I have ever met. She had long chestnut hair, Isabella's aristocratic nose, and almond eyes. She was always smiling, and was terribly in love with Mr. Albero. It was a total tragedy when she died of breast cancer when we were twelve."

Jade, Isabella's oldest and best friend had attended the same middle school as Isabella. She remembered bringing over dinners that her mom, Sloan, had made for the Albero family during the illness of

Isabella's mother. When Sharon Rose died, the whole eighth grade class attended.

"Mrs. A's dying wish to her daughter was that she save herself for marriage and true love." Jade said, wistfully.

Cyrus asked, "I guess her mom was of the old school and very religious?"

Jade answered, "Not really, she was artsy, always designing and sewing outfits. She made beautiful costumes for us; lovely Halloween outfits, and beautiful dresses. She was romantic and loved flowers, and was always reading poetry or sketching. But, on the topic of why the request, I do have an idea." Jade commented.

"One day, Mrs. Albero pulled me aside. I've never told anyone about this, not even Isabella. Mrs. A., Sharon Rose, she said that it was not going to be an easy road for her daughter. She said that Isabella would need loyal friends who respected her being different. And, Mrs. A. knew that because I was different than my peers, that I would understand what she meant."

"Jade, you are an interesting and special person, but, in what way did Mrs. Albero mean that you are different?" asked a curious Cyrus.

"Well, my mom is African American, and my dad is Jewish. That's different. In Ardmore, where I was from, I was one of the only girls of mixed race. Now, being biracial isn't all that unusual; we've even got a president who is like me but in the reverse. But in my neighborhood, it was very unusual.

Jade explained that Ardmore was populated by descendents of the workers of the old time Main Line mansions, and that it was a very stable, thriving black community.

"Anyway, Mrs. Albero wanted me to be supportive of Isabella being "different" – and, at the time, I thought she meant that Isabella had a sick mother. But, after her mother died, Isabella told me about the deathbed promise," explained Jade.

"Oh, and she also said something about learning about life the hard way. That she, Sharon Rose, had learned about things the hard way and she wanted things to be easier for her daughter. That is ironic though, because it has been way tough on her to be different."

"So, Jade, enough about your BFF." Cyrus cooed, in a friendly way, "Tell me about you, I want to know everything," Jade said.

The rest of the evening was spent getting to know each other in a cozy setting. Cyrus kept a significant part of his research on Isabella to himself. What he knew about women, gleaned from being the youngest in a family of three sisters, and being the subject of a lot of female attention, kept him from full disclosure. Best friends always share everything, there was no holding back. He was counting on Jade tipping Isabella off to the fact that she was a suspect in his investigation of the bizarre deliveries and notes. However, he wanted to keep some other, more shocking, information to himself until he was able to sort it out more fully. For now, he would just enjoy Jade's company, and delight in the fact that they have more in common than he had earlier supposed.

Chapter 26 - Gaining Ground

"No landscaping task is too big or too small for Lanzetti."
Company motto

It was Thursday, and Patrick and Isabella had returned to the Ames building to take a better look at the rooftop, as it was a little drizzly on their first visit. They brought a digital camera to take photographs, needed to take some additional measurements of the roof, and to ask a few questions.

Ennis was happy to let them into the rooftop, and he took a route that included the main stairwell and not the service entrance.

"Do you always treat your hired help so graciously?" Patrick enquired.

"Hardly." Ennis murmured. "If you weren't here, I'd be taking the service entrance myself."

Isabella and Patrick looked at each other with confusion.

Ennis said, "I mean, I am just doing what my boss told me to do."

"Mrs. Crescent?" Isabella asked.

Ennis laughed. "Her? Oh, she's the housekeeper. She does make a lot of decisions for the boss, though. They trust her lots because she's worked here for decades." Ennis thought to himself, Amy was here back when the boss liked women, or so he'd been told. Now, that is something he would like to have seen. Alistair was a proud, happy member of the alternative lifestyle contingency, not that there is anything wrong with that, Ennis mused.

"And who does she work for?" Patrick prompted, thinking that this was rather mysterious.

"Well, the apartment *is* called the Ames Building, right?" said Ennis. "Do folks from Pennsylvania always ask so many questions?"

Once they were lead to the rooftop, Ennis sat on a chair to rehearse his lines for his next audition, while they were left to do their design preparations.

"Isabella, I need to stretch my legs, would you mind walking the steps with me a minute...You know me, I'm used to the big outdoors. It gets stuffy here in the city, even on a rooftop with this great skyline."

"Really, Pat, you're like a caged animal sometimes," answered Isabella, going along with what was probably a not-so-subtle way to speak privately about the mysterious goings on at the Ames.

"Have you been given any other contact information for Ms. Crescent or the Ames family?" Pat asked when they were safely in the stairwell.

"Well, just an e-mail address and...wait, yes, there's a fax number here."

Pat ran a reverse directory search on his iPhone, and the listing was for the basement floor of the Ames building.

The number was ascribed to by one, Laura C. Ames. Yes, indeed, this Laura was the sort of person who owned not just the penthouse and the roof of a building of this magnitude, but *the entire building*.

Maneuvering from the steps to the rooftop down through the service entrance, then down to the basement, Pat was enjoying himself immensely. This adventure sure beat snow removal, the least favorite of his tasks, he mused.

His grandfather, Lance, had built Lanzetti Landscaping, operating out of their one-acre family home in Devon, over 45 years ago. Upon his graduation from State College, he had assumed all aspects of design for the family business. However, there were times when he had to take whatever odd job was unaccounted for, which was one of the drawbacks of working for family. However, this physical labor had made him sleek and strong, and his muscles bulging.

Pat used a tender caress to pull a stray hair back from Isabella's forehead, and said, "Isabella, do you want to meet the wizard behind the screen here?"

A few minutes later, Isabella was walking into the staff only area of the Ames building, owned by Mrs. Ames, widow of the Ames family fortune.

"Lord, Ennis aren't you supposed to be up on the roof?" asked an agitated Mrs. Crescent. After looking up and seeing Pete and Isabella, she fainted clear onto the floor.

With the maid dressed in the black and white get-up held firmly in his arms, Pat pushed open the door labeled "kitchenette."

Not finding anyone about, Isabella found a sink and put some water on a towel to apply to Mrs. Crescent's forehead.

"You seem to have had quite an effect on this woman," drawled Isabella, as she tried to make sense out of the situation.

"No, Isabella, it was after seeing you that she fainted. But that is neither heads nor tails. She could be having some sort of seizure. Or, this could be another understudy practicing her lines. Come to think of it, that was a stunning faint."

The maid, who looked to be around 55, started to stir. She blinked a few times and said, "Rosie, is that you?"

Mrs. Crescent, upon reviving, apologized for fainting. She said that she hadn't had anything for breakfast that day. Then, she asked to see Isabella.

As Isabella walked closer, Mrs. Crescent exclaimed, "Aren't you the spitting image of your mama, and..." she looked closer for further inspection, "and just as pretty. Why, if I didn't know any better, I would think it was Rose. I remember when she modeled for that jeans ad with the flower petals, you know, the one in 'Haute'...."

"Thank you, but you must be mistaken. My mother wasn't into haute couture; she was all about horticulture, as in gardening. Her name was Sharon Rose Albero; she lived in Wynnewood, Pennsylvania, where she helped my father tend the grounds and she darned his socks. You must be thinking of someone else entirely." Isabella said.

"Why my dear, your mother was like a sister to me. We lived downstairs, here at the Ames building. She was a model, you know. And I, well, I was a singer. But, that is neither here nor there. I have to tell you, I am so happy to know that she had a happy family." Mrs. Crescent was clearly touched at meeting the daughter of one of her dearest friends.

"I am sorry, but you are totally mistaken. I am from a family of gardeners, and, my mom sewed Halloween costumes and things. She was a homemaker. Well, like, you know how the Von Trappe family sang? Well, we gardened. That was our thing. I don't even think my mom was ever in New York, she always said it was too crowded and polluted." Isabella was getting more and more agitated.

"Isabella," interjected Patrick, "Let's go back up to the roof and complete our photo taking and measuring for the, uh, design. We are sorry to have disturbed you, Mrs. Crescent. I hope you are feeling better and that you have a good rest of the day."

Patrick drove the truck the whole way back to the Main Line with very little in the way of conversation. He knew when to keep his mouth shut and to allow other people to work through their own thoughts in an amiable silence.

When Pat dropped off a confused Isabella at her twin "Wayne Dog" rented apartment, he asked her if she would be alright.

"Of course, nothing is wrong. Why are you asking?" asked a defensive Isabella. "That lady doesn't know what she's talking about. She must have done too many drugs in the '60's, I feel sad for her."

"Ok, well, let me know if you need anything," Pat said, as he left. "I'll be at Casper's in Berwyn," mentioning a local tavern, "in case you need me."

Isabella went inside and took a shower to relax. It didn't work. She got dressed and dried her hair, but she kept thinking about this "Rosie." "Impossible," she uttered, as she thought that her mother could have had another life in the Big Apple.

"OK, I'll just take a little look," she said, as she booted up the outdated computer that sat at her desk. "This darned thing always takes so long to log on." Isabella grumbled.

Her first search was for "Haute Magazine" and "jeans ad" and "rose petals" and nothing came up. But, she decided that the first word would be "Ames," plus the other search words.

"Open to the public, retrospective of the works of famed photographer and photo-journalist, Jacqui Nachman. Nachman's works include woodlands restoration and other environmental topics, as well as the glorious photographs of jeans advertisements in Haute magazine spanning 3 decades."

"My favorite of the jeans advertisements," Nachman says in the interview preceding the retrospective, "was an obscure one from the 1970s. A beautiful new model named Karen, or was it Sharon, I don't remember, anyway, she said that her middle name was Rose. I liked that, and it sort of went with it for the theme of the shot. Sporting rose petals on her midriff, she was so carefree and full of spunk - a real firebrand. I think she was the publisher's sister or girlfriend or something. I don't know whatever became of her, but I really loved her spirit, it was so effervescent and she was just willing to do anything, totally carefree and uninhibited."

Accompanying the article covering the retrospective and the interview was a small reprint of the Haute ad with the caption, "The Photographers Favorite."

While the photo was very small, Isabella was able to save it to the server and then enlarge it on the computer.

She had no doubt who she was looking at, and it was startling. Where was Jade? She needed to find her right now to help sort this all out.

Jade knew she was being a high-maintenance girlfriend by stopping over to Cyrus' pad, unannounced, the day after their magical date.

However, she had a really good excuse to intrude. He had taken her iPad without meaning to, and she needed it for work. Wow, that sounded really good, if only she could pull it off without sounding sort of like she was desperate to see him again and planted it in his jacket pocket.

Well, serves him right for wearing blazers in the summer, she thought.

As she knocked on the door to the gatehouse of the Albero Estate, Jade recalled the last time she had been there, back when it was the residence of the Albero family. Now, it was the place where Cyrus lived while he was guarding Max on this coast.

Suddenly, her cell phone rang. It was Isabella desperately wanting to see Jade on an urgent matter. It couldn't wait; Isabella needed to see her right away. Jade told her best friend where she was, at Isabella's childhood home, and told her to come there right away.

Chapter 27 - A Dip In The Pool

"Don't stop!"
Isabella to Max at the swimming pool of the Ivy Estates

By the time Isabella drove to the gatehouse from her apartment, it was dark. Her eyes were red, obviously from crying.

Cyrus, the youngest son in a family with three girls, was immediately keen on the situation. He would allow Jade and Isabella use of the gatehouse, and said that he would sleep at the main house that night. There were guest toiletries and some nightclothes he found in the back of the closet, Cyrus explained.

Upon inspection, Isabella realized that these nightdresses were sewn by, and worn by, her mother.

As Jade fell asleep in the master bedroom, Isabella tossed and turned in her childhood bedroom. The sheets felt hot, she felt overheated.

There had to be something that could cool her off. She decided to take a walk around the estate, and she took a flashlight with her to help see, although she knew her way around the estate like the back of her hand.

She found herself next to the swimming pool, a place that she had been strictly told never to go to as a child.

She walked over to the chaise lounges next to the shallow end of the pool.

"I guess I won't need these," Isabella commented, as she threw off her nightgown and her shoes.

It was a warm, humid September night, and she was alone at the swimming pool.

Jade was sleeping, and Isabella thought that she would use this time to catch up on all of the naughty things she had missed out on all these years.

First on the list would be skinny-dipping in the Ivy pool.

As a child, she had been mesmerized by the sight of the pool, but only was able to be near it when her father was tending to the grounds near the pool.

This was it for living life from afar, thought Isabella. From now on, she was going to live life in the fast lane.

For so many years, she had asked herself, when in a difficult situation, what her mother would have done.

Now, she was unfettered.

Sharon Rose, or Rosie as she was known in Manhattan, would have done just about anything and everything, evidently. And she did!

"Carpe diem" would be her daughter's new motto.

The pool was a vintage style with art deco tiles surrounding it. It featured rare and unusual carvings along the wall facing the changing cabanas. There was even an outdoor kitchen for cookouts. These Ivy's had everything.

Well, clearly, someone ought to be enjoying this tempting, tantalizing water retreat. Those Ivy's were probably all in the Hamptons visiting with the other Main Line Brahmans. That is, except Max.

Isabella, sure to stay in the shallow end, took a few steps down. She enjoyed the feeling of the water trailing along her body.

She had decided to keep her skivvies on, which, were actually quite like a pink bikini swimsuit, come to think of it. They were a recent hand-me-down from Marissa, and Isabella could see why they would not fit her anymore, now that her friend was breastfeeding baby Ivy.

Yes, Max and Cyrus were probably the only ones in that big stately mansion, she thought. Recollecting the time in Jimmy's yard that Max brushed up against her as he showed her some stretches to do before gardening, she recalled the feeling of his body next to hers. That was a delicious sensation, and something she fully intended on exploring.

Continuing to walk, and preoccupied with thoughts of getting closer to Max, she ended up in a part of the pool that quickly dipped from four to six feet.

She was trying to jump up where the air was, hoping to take a few breaths while she returned the other way. Quickly, and before panic set in, two large arms supported her as the life float was set underneath her arm pit.

It was a rescue right out of the lifeguard TV show, *Babeview*, which was where Max had seen the necessary rescue moves.

Isabella seemed to be breathing on her own, thank God. As Max lifted her out of the water and took her over to a patch of grass, he was surprised at her skimpy swimming apparel.

"Did you get a leg cramp or something?" he asked.

"Can't swim, never learned, feel like a fool, don't even ask." She said, between gasps for air.

"I'm so glad you're OK, I don't know how I knew to come out here," Max explained.

Isabella interrupted him with a sudden request, "Shut up and kiss me."

Max, who had been dreaming of doing just that for many, many months, was happy to comply. But, he felt that he needed to make sure that he wasn't taking advantage of the situation, or the girl. He wanted to be a true gentleman.

"Are you sure?" Max started to ask.

Just as he was completing the sentence, Isabella kissed him with total abandon.

She molded herself perfectly to his contours, like they were made for each other. She started to kiss him on his neck, and then on his bare chest. She was feeling very naughty, indeed.

Her nubile, sensual form clung to him in total surrender. "Please just take me, all of me," she implored.

At this point, Max was having a little talk with the angel on one shoulder and the devil on the other.

The former was imploring him to take it slow, not to forget that she almost drowned, and to give her some time to sleep on this. The latter was thinking about the best place and the best way to give her what she wanted when she wanted it.

"Isabella," he said, "I would like that very much. I have thought about it many times. But, your first time should be in a bed, with romantic music, candlelight, and fresh strawberries and cream. It should be with someone you really care about and want a real relationship with, and we all know what you think of me."

Isabella had just been thoroughly kissed and was thinking that it would be nice to get back to that. She was not much in the mood for a chat.

"Shut up and kiss me," she retorted.

Max knew that this was what she wanted, and it seemed like a great place to start, so he kissed her gladly.

As he brushed his tongue against her teeth, he heard a sensuous whimper in response. "Don't stop!" she said, breathlessly.

He thought about how responsive she was to his kisses, and knew that they would have a great chemistry in bed. That reminded him of the bed, and he knew where he wanted this to go.

"Isabella, I want to give you some time to think about this. I am going to go back to the main house to wait for you. It will take about an hour for me to create the right atmosphere; light some candles, put some classical music on, and have a fresh fruit bowl next to the bed. Your first time deserves some scenery and some specialness. If you change your mind, I'll understand. And, when things are going on with us, if you change your mind, just let me know. One of the advantages to my being, uh, rather experienced is that I have a lot of control over myself." Max explained.

Isabella walked with Max to see the outside entrance to his room. She asked, "If you are so experienced, can I ask if you are also safe?"

Max looked at her and said, "I've been tested, if that is what you mean. And, in the last few years I have been very selective and exclusive. It was only in college that I was "Boys Gone Wild" and all. Things have really toned down for me personally, even though professionally I *am* hot stuff."

 "And modest, too," she giggled.

"Isabella, right now I am *very insecure*. I'm not sure if it is really *me* that you want, or just the first available guy who can rock your world, and all. I want to know that this is what you really want. That's why we need this time to think. I'll respect you whatever decision you make."

As Isabella started on the path back to the gatehouse, she wondered about the expression "the one." Was there really a right person for everyone? How would she know that Max was "the one"? It all was so much easier when she was going to join the convent.

And that's when they both heard a loud scream…

Afterword

This is far from being the end of Isabella and Max's story; it is only the beginning. Their relationship continues in Prune, Plant, or Plunder: Part II - Isabella's Petals. Coming in 2012!